WELCOME
TO PARADISE

WELCOME TO PARADISE

MAHI BINEBINE

Translated by Lulu Norman

Tin House Books

Portland, Oregon & New York, New York

First published in France as *Cannibales* by Librairie Artheme
Fayard 1999

First published in Great Britain by Granta Books 2003

First North American edition published by Tin House Books 2012

Published by Tin House Books, Portland, Oregon, and
New York, New York

Distributed to the trade by Publishers Group West, 1700 Fourth St.,
Berkeley, CA 94710, www.pgw.com

Library of Congress Cataloging-in-Publication Data

Binebine, Mahi.
  [Cannibales. English]
  Welcome to paradise / Mahi Binebine ; translated by Lulu Norman. —
1st North American ed.
    p. cm.
  ISBN 978-1-935639-27-5 (trade paper) — ISBN 978-1-935639-28-2
(ebook)
  1. Immigrants—Fiction. 2. Refugees—Fiction. 3. Morocco—
Fiction. I. Norman, Lulu. II. Title.
  PQ3989.2.B534C3613 2012
  843'.914—dc23

                              2012002454

Interior design by Diane Chonette
Printed in the USA
www.tinhouse.com

For Agustin and Bâ titi, who must be laughing now

Mahi Binebine's Invisible Men

HOW SHALL I introduce the Moroccan author Mahi Binebine? I'll introduce him to you the way I encountered him myself—through this small but evocative novel, *Welcome to Paradise*, and then in person, during the PEN World Voices Festival in New York in the spring of 2011.

I first heard about *Welcome to Paradise* when it came out in England in 2003 and was short-listed for the Independent Foreign Fiction Prize. (It was originally published in French with the more ominous title *Cannibales*.) "Sober and unsentimental, *Welcome to Paradise* is a highly moving homage to the new wretched of the earth," wrote *Le Monde*. "Mahi Binebine is the first Moroccan writer to give these lives an identity," added *El Pais*. I was intrigued—who was this author and exactly whose lives was he seeking to rescue from obscurity?

I read the book in anticipation of our conversation for the PEN festival, and I was struck immediately by the rhythm of Binebine's storytelling voice, its gentle push and pull, rocking back and forth in time like a rickety boat at sea. Indeed, this is a story of the sea, though it is set completely on shore, along the sands, cafés, and villages of Morocco that are transfixed by the view of Spain in the distance. "Back in the village, the old people were always telling us about the sea, and each time in a different way," Aziz, the narrator, explains in the book's opening lines. "Some said it was like a vast sky, a sky of water foaming across infinite, impenetrable forests where ghosts and ferocious monsters lived."

For Aziz and the rest of a small group of hopeful illegal immigrants, the sea represents many things at once—a threshold to another world, a dark mystery, a cruel joke. As they huddle along its edge over the course of the book's one long night, Binebine delicately, patiently, spins their individual tales to reveal how they've arrived at this fateful moment with their lives entrusted to a cagey trafficker, one small boat, and the fickle, treacherous sea.

Here are the characters whose sad, finely etched stories Binebine is so intent on bringing to life: there is Aziz's cousin, Reda, still wracked with guilt and terror by the memory of his mother's suicide; the Algerian Kacem Judi, who's escaped the trauma of his country's civil war, though without his children; Nuara, in search of the father of her baby, who's vanished into the mythic streets of Paris; and Pafadnam, a "colossus" from Mali who is bent over with "the air of someone apologizing for existing." And even more cruel twists and devastations are revealed: a mute twin whose infected hands must be amputated; a father who unwittingly steals rice laced with rat poison, which results in dire consequences for his entire family.

But if this all sounds unrelentingly grim, it isn't—or at least not entirely. Perhaps because these stories are told in reflection, the aches are dulled and the book is imbued instead with a feverish, if misguided, optimism, an unshakable vision of a future "paradise" just across the shore. Aziz and the others are all finally so close—but close to what? "One more hour and we could shrug off our mud-caked memories," sighs Aziz, "drive the adobe hovels out of our minds, forget the barren fields, the life of struggle, poverty, and distress. One hour, Lord, just one little hour, and, eyes closed, we'd be carried away on the tides of this forbidden dream."

Theirs is not only a forbidden dream, however; it is also a risky and potentially fatal one that is ignored by much of the wider world. And in order to realize this dream, they become truly nameless and stateless, burying their identity papers along the beach. The actors of *Welcome to Paradise* are, for the most part, unseen and too easily discounted on both sides of the watery divide. "The world went on turning. No one bothered about us, it was as if we didn't exist, as if we'd never been born," Aziz realizes. "So come on, honestly, what did it matter if we were devoured here, or somewhere else, or on the open seas?"

And so this is also a book about invisibility, about the oblivion of Africa's poor and rootless in the early years of the twenty-first century. These are Binebine's "new" wretched of the earth, his "shadow people." And like the stooped and defeated Pafadnam, they're prepared for a life in the West, where, despite the rosy picture painted by Morad, the "European Deportee" who negotiated their passage, they'll need to learn how to

> disappear into a crowd, hug the walls, avoid eye contact, speak only when spoken to, bury [their] pride and close [their] hearts to humiliation and insults, throw [their] switchblades in the gutter, learn to keep in the background, to be nobody: another shadow, a stray dog, a lowly earthworm, or even a cockroach. That's it, yes, learn to be a cockroach.

In person, not surprisingly, Binebine's storytelling voice is as rich and layered as his writing, though more rollicking and frequently punctuated by a hearty belly laugh. He is what would be called an old-fashioned raconteur, though he's from a land where the "storytellers of Marrakesh" are legendary and the art of verbal embroidery has never gone out of fashion. Binebine is the first to say his stories come from the cafés and streets of Marrakesh, his home city, from news flashes and rumors, passed-down tall tales and family lore. "When you're a writer, you're a sponge," he told me during our festival program. "I go to the cafés in Marrakesh and people come up to me and tell me their stories. If you want to be a writer, you really have to know how to listen."

He told me too of his other books, also drawn as if from the day's headlines. There's the one he likens to a "Shakespearean" saga, based on his brother's attempted coup against the former king of Morocco, whose trusted aide was their own father, and how the brother survived more than twenty years in the country's most notorious prison; a lighter, more comic novel about hippies and Moroccan poppy fields; and his latest, *The Stars of Sidi Moumen*, which explores the experiences of child suicide bombers seeking their own eternal "paradise" as an escape from the slums of Casablanca. (Tin House will release *The Stars of Sidi Moumen* in April 2013, the tenth anniversary of the actual Casablanca attack.)

And then there is his artwork, for he is a world-renowned visual artist as well. The two worlds, literary and artistic, complement and converge, much as his drawings of expressive faces entwine and blend together powerfully in his signature paintings. His books, he explained, move from the inside out, from the personal to the social-political, while his art strives to draw you from the outside in. (When I asked which he had wanted to become first, a writer or an artist, he blurted out, "A singer!")

We met, as I mentioned, in late April 2011, so the North African uprisings of the "Arab Spring"—which spread from Tunisia to Egypt and Libya, but for a variety of reasons largely eluded Morocco—were still echoing in our minds. Binebine, for one, was humbled, and excited. "These are truly extraordinary revolutions!" he exclaimed. "These are revolutions of the young against being crushed, against being humiliated!" By the week's end there would be a terrorist attack on a familiar Marrakesh café, and Binebine was called upon to comment on events for a range of foreign newspapers. He was clearly shaken: this was where he himself sat and drew on the life around him for material. This was where he heard the stories of the anonymous and forgotten lives that he turned into literature. "These people, even when they get to Spain, are considered shadows, phantoms," he said of the characters of *Welcome to Paradise*, returning to his underlying theme. "They don't exist; they're hiding. What I hoped to do with this book was give them an identity, a history."

So there you have it—a literary introduction of sorts to a book, but something more than that as well, I hope: a full-bodied glimpse of its author, Mahi Binebine, dripping with paint and compassion, with a bellowing laugh and seemingly endless source of life stories, and an entry into his world. Now read this book and take the journey with him so that you, too, will know of what he speaks.

—ANDERSON TEPPER

1

BACK IN THE village, the old people were always telling us about the sea, and each time in a different way. Some said it was like a vast sky, a sky of water foaming across infinite, impenetrable forests where ghosts and ferocious monsters lived. Others maintained that it stretched farther than all the rivers, lakes, ponds, and streams on earth put together. As for the wise old boys in the square, who spoke as one on the matter, they swore that God was storing up that water for Judgment Day, when it would wash the earth clean of sinners.

It was dark and there was a faint mist. Hidden behind a rock, we could hear the sound of the wind and the waves. Morad had said the sea was calm at that time of year and we'd believed him. We'd believe anything as long as it meant we could get away—as far away as possible, and for good.

A black shadow hovered near the boat. It was the trafficker. We didn't know his name, we just called him "Boss" with a kind of fearful deference, the way you might a teacher brandishing a cane, a cruel-eyed policeman, a wizard casting spells, or anyone that holds your future in his hands. From time to time, strange grunts emerged from his turned-down hood.

I wasn't sure if it was the fear or the cold that was making my cousin Reda shiver. Both, maybe. We were all cold and frightened, but Reda seemed to have it worst. His face looked pale and strained, he was hugging his Adidas bag to his chest and his teeth were chattering. Nonstop. He'd just lit a cigarette when the shadow swooped and grabbed it, and stuck it in his mouth. Reda didn't even react, he just kept on shivering and his teeth kept chattering. Near me, Nuara was nursing her baby. I couldn't work out how old she was from her round, plumpish face. Crowned with tightly plaited hair, her head was rocking to the rhythm of a silent lullaby. A breast hung slackly from her blouse. I stared at it, my eyes glued to the nipple in the minuscule mouth. The baby, whose bawling we dreaded, was kneading it in his tiny little hands. The trafficker had made no bones about it: "Any noise, one mistake, and this'll be a living hell for all of us." But good God, what hell could that be? Was there a deeper, blacker one than the one poverty had cast us into?

Apart from us four, there was Kacem Judi, an Algerian from Blida who'd been a teacher in the days when his country was at peace, Pafadnam and Yarcé, two Malians visible only by the whites of their eyes, and Yussef, who said he came from Marrakesh but whose thick accent sounded

Berber to me, probably from the Middle Atlas. It seemed calm enough, our little group. Pafadnam, who was so big he was like a giant, was on his third go. Why did he have to tell us? Only the night before, in the café, Morad, the trafficker's partner, had assured us that crossing the Strait of Gibraltar never took more than a few hours. "It's not a trip to the moon," he'd joked.

I had laughed, but Reda had not. He had a dreadful stomachache, which made him get up from the table every quarter of an hour, only to come back just as pale as he'd left. Morad, whose short, cocky build, carefully groomed appearance, and macabre sense of humor reminded us of the Spaniards in Tangier, had warned us, "If that idiot keeps on getting the shits, we're throwing him overboard!" At this, my cousin had practically fainted and things had taken a turn for the worse. Suddenly there was a pestilential stink, and everyone was backing away from the table. Everyone except me, of course. It was stifling in the café. The Moroccan national orchestra was cranking out a patriotic song on the radio and the blue ceiling was hidden behind a veil of kif and tobacco smoke. Reda didn't dare move. He stayed perched on the edge of his seat, hands clamped to the arms of the plastic chair. Tentative at first, the grumbling from the nearby tables grew nastier as the stink spread, until finally it alerted the waiter, who ran up, foaming at the mouth, like a wild animal whose territory's been soiled. Instantly sniffing out the situation, he began to yell at the top of his voice. I stood up and stuck out my chest, ready to put a stop to his insults, but seeing I only came up to his shoulder, I changed my tune.

"This young man is ill, sir!"

"I'm not his mother, you scumbag!" he cursed, grabbing Reda by the collar of his shirt. I tried to step between them and took a blow to the chin, which left me stunned for a moment, so instead I followed them outside. An abrupt silence had fallen over the terrace, everyone was staring at us. The café waiter, whose shrill voice sounded ridiculous coming from his hulking frame, pushed Reda ahead of him, hurling abuse. A trickle of urine came after. Someone sniggered, then someone else, and the whole terrace erupted. Reda wasn't doing anything. He seemed far away, letting himself be put out like the garbage. Spurred on by the customers' gibes, the waiter triumphantly crowned his bravery with a vicious kick that sent my cousin sprawling into the gutter.

I didn't like seeing Reda on the ground. I'd never been able to bear it. As kids, back in the village, everyone, even the puniest boy in our gang, used to beat him up. Whenever the slightest quarrel broke out, he'd panic and be paralyzed with fear. He'd hunch up, using his arms to protect his face, and wait for me to come to the rescue. I always would. It often cost me, but I was always there to defend him, because Reda is my blood. So, in front of this terrace full of layabouts, shoeshine boys, kids renting out newspapers, petty crooks, corrupt civil servants, and other complete nobodies, I bent down and picked up *my blood*.

I didn't even deign to insult that barbarian rabble, though my throat seethed with curses heaven had rarely heard. If they'd caught even a glimmer of the hate and scorn that glittered in my eyes, they'd have stopped laughing and pointing. Because a man from the South, humiliated as I was, is an unpredictable man, capable of the craziest things.

Staggering slightly, Reda leaned his full weight on me, his arm round my shoulder, his head lolling forward. We walked away slowly, in silence. I'd have liked to tell him the terrible forms my vengeance would take. That bastard's got it coming, I'll have him, you'll see. I've got plans for him . . . an ambush . . . at night . . . some dark alley. He won't see a thing. Lucky I held on to my switchblade; little brother was dying to get his hands on it, wasn't he! (I almost gave it to him before we left. The little monkey had woken at dawn and was standing there, by the dusty lorry that was taking Reda and me north. He looked at me, his eyes all shining, not asking for anything, but I knew how desperate he was for that knife.) See, I was right not to give in. You should always keep your knife on you. I'll make that bastard bleed; he's big, but I'll take him by surprise; I'll slash his face, give him an almighty scar to remember me by . . . This is a son of Tassaout you're dealing with here. Believe it.

So I carried on plotting bloody revenge, but Reda never knew. He walked beside me, his arms dangling, his bag slung across his chest. We headed for the street pump— a bit of a cleanup was looking pretty urgent. No offense to him, but my cousin stank like rotting meat. The grilled sardines we'd forced down at midday near the port must have had something to do with it. Anyway, the ridiculous price should have tipped me off. Still, I pretended I couldn't smell anything. The setting sun cast a peachy glow over the walls, the shops, the animals, and people as we walked, and the pump wasn't much farther. Some snotty-nosed kids were playing round it. It was not a reassuring sight; I knew what that scabby mob could do if they caught Reda having a quiet wash in the middle of the street. I knew exactly how ferocious they could be. When I was a kid, God forgive me, a beggar coming to wash at the pump was pure heaven for us. We'd lie in wait like cats until he had his ass in the air, then leap out and put him through all the miseries known to man. We'd steal his bundle or his skullcap or we'd tug at his hood, making him fall over backward. That was the funniest sight on earth. To see him soaked to the skin with his trousers round his ankles and no way of running after us, frothing with rage, ranting and cursing, had us in complete ecstasy. We'd roll on the ground, splitting our sides with laughter. We'd clap our hands, shouting victory to the skies. But now, in this putrid, muggy dusk, with my pitiful cousin in his pitiful state, laughing was the last thing on my mind.

We sat down by the pump, without speaking, without even looking at each other, and, huddled together like two lost beggars, waited patiently for night to fall.

2

"WHAT ARE THOSE lights over there?" Reda asked.

A gust of wind sprayed us with damp sand, making everyone shudder.

"That's Spain, isn't it? Isn't that Spain?"

Nobody was in a chatting mood.

"Morad did say that on clear nights you could see . . ."

"Shut up!" growled the trafficker.

"If paradise were that close, son," murmured the Algerian, "I'd have swum there by now."

We all smiled.

Reda felt emboldened: "So what are those lights then?"

"They're lightships," said the Algerian, as if he were an authority on all things illegal.

Reda stared goggle-eyed.

"A lightship is a floating beacon, son, which gives sailors their bearings, important ones. But that makes it dangerous."

"Dangerous?"

"Deadly sometimes. The coastguard are often lurking nearby. And those bastards'll sometimes imitate the light-ships by turning their searchlights so they shine straight up at the sky; the novice smugglers get drawn in like moths."

Reda's teeth set to chattering again. His complexion turned green, making me dread another explosion from the gut area.

The sea spray and the sand kept up their attack, whip-ping our faces at regular intervals. The rock that sheltered us wasn't very high; I didn't see why we couldn't have picked another one.

Leaning against the boat, which lay upturned on the sand, dressed in an incongruous three-piece suit, the Algerian began to explain in a reassuring voice that an experienced smuggler would never fall for such childish tricks. And, judging by his appearance and composure, our gracious Savior looked a proper seadog. Look how he's scanning the sky, you can tell he understands the language of the stars. Believe you me, he's a past master in the art of reading the night. Oh, you have to be an artist as well to do this job, my children, a true artist!

Having made several attempts to cross, Kacem Judi knew what he was talking about. And they'd have been successful, too, if it weren't for the rotten luck that clung to him, if, like most of his countrymen, he weren't cursed by the gods—he, Kacem Judi, the survivor of the butchery at Blida. Because bad luck is like lice: once it takes hold, it's very hard to get rid of. Not that it had affected his longing to escape; he'd always come through his countless adventures unscathed. And this time, he could feel it in his bones, this was going to be the one . . .

Just when we were least expecting it, because he seemed to be asleep, the baby started bawling. Very loudly.

Back in the village, we have a house made of mud and spit, with two furnished rooms (grass mats, sheepskins, and cushions); a stable housing one scrawny cow, two goats, and an old she-ass; and a small yard mainly taken up by a large well with adobe. Doors are rough woollen blankets woven by my mother. I'm the eldest of eight brothers and sisters. In other words, no stranger to screaming kids. But this little maniac's crying took my breath away: it was a shrill, sharp, siren wail; quite impressive for such a wisp of a thing. The shadow stirred and gave another grunt. Reda's teeth, which had only just stopped chattering, started up again. Nuara struggled to comfort her boy with exaggerated rocking movements, humming a tune that made the little mite cry more instead of calming him down.

The pressure mounted: on tenterhooks, we waited for the trafficker's verdict. There was going to be one, and from such a prickly individual we knew it would be harsh. But he was taking his time, while the bawling grew louder. I was keeping an eye on Reda, whose courage could have deserted him at any moment that night. Kacem Judi was cleaning his nails with a Swiss army knife, just like one I'd been given by a tourist I'd shown around for a few days.

Salvation eventually came from Yarcé, the Malian who up until then hadn't uttered a word.

He was a timid, unassuming little fellow; we'd almost forgotten he was there, so buried was he in darkness and silence, a shadow among the night's shadows.

"Just put him under the boat and let's be done with it!" he muttered, as naturally as could be. At first the suggestion seemed absurd, cruel, but on second thoughts it wasn't so foolish. Yussef even backed him up, saying that under the boat the baby would be out of the cold and damp that were chilling us to the bone. The argument sank in, we weighed the pros and cons, and still hesitated. But when the trafficker turned to Nuara with a determined look, we all agreed the plan was worthwhile, sensible, and in the end, the only option.

At first the young woman shook her head; she hugged her child to her and tried to give him the breast again. Then, slowly getting to her feet, she fixed her pleading eyes on ours, which were lowered but unyielding, and then, without a word, she took to her heels and vanished into the dark. She didn't run far, poor thing. We were a long way from the city, in a deserted, lifeless place with hostile cliffs, gusting sand, and just the melancholy echo of the odd drunk and a few nocturnal seagulls trailing an invisible trawler. The safest thing was to stay with us, Nuara knew that, which was why she came back a little later, looking sheepish, her head bowed, heralded by the shrieking of her offspring.

"I'm not leaving my baby alone under there," she said, in a strangled voice. "If you let me, I'll go in with him."

She knelt down, her trembling hands gripping her baby tight enough to suffocate him.

"Now there's a wise decision!" exclaimed Yussef.

Our anxious glances all rested on the trafficker, who acted as if he hadn't noticed a thing. He was wearing an enormous green oilskin with the hood lowered over his face like a cowl, which made him look like a sea ghost. His agreement, when it came, was a huge relief. A chorus of sighs greeted the outcome and again we praised Yarcé's suggestion. He'd already shrunk back into himself, miles away from everything.

Four of us got in position to lift the boat, which weighed a ton. Mother and child slipped underneath and lay down on a snarl of ropes, and we lowered the hull, taking care not to crush them. The effect was instantaneous and unexpected: the baby immediately fell silent and Nuara stopped sniffling. Flashing his silver teeth, the trafficker turned to the Malian and nodded. Though jealous, we all did the same. It was the first time our gracious Savior had shown a trace of human warmth, and we were inordinately grateful for that small gesture, as if he'd granted some extraordinary boon. Yussef went so far as to hold out his hand, which the trafficker declined; after all, courtesy had its limits.

What had happened underneath the boat? Kacem Judi, who had a detailed explanation for just about everything, declared that mother and child had simply gone out like a light and sunk into a deep sleep, as any of us would have done. I had a different take on it, although the Algerian wasn't really wrong; we were all so exhausted that we could have gone straight to sleep in the roughest conditions. But for me this upturned boat on the sand prompted strange thoughts, images without beginning or end, a parade of fantasies I couldn't get out of my head. Yes, that boat covering living souls made me think of a giant coffin, a bottomless box open to the shades below. I saw the earth pregnant with a mother nursing her child, life and death joined in the same, lonely silence. I saw the sand breathing, the night conspiring. Mother and baby warm and dry, their hearts at peace, huddled together in the dark pit of a stomach, where the roar of the sea sounded, as in a shell. Were they still alive? Had they tasted the first fruits of that bliss my grandfather used to speak of, that ineffable peace on the banks of everlasting night? Whatever the truth of it, for hours on end and until the first barking of the dogs, no one heard them so much as twitch.

3

IT WAS AFTER ten. We were still in the same place, numb with fear and cold, sodden, worn out physically as much as mentally. The day had been long, the evening longer still. The waves pounded relentlessly against the reefs and breakwaters; I could feel them breaking in my veins. Reda had fallen asleep on my shoulder with his mouth open, his jaw slack. The wind was dropping, which had encouraged Pafadnam to take out his meal of barley bread, black olives, and fried fish. It smelled good. Kacem Judi had produced a tomato salad, some meatballs, and a navel orange; Yarcé, a sandwich—I couldn't make out what was in it. As for Yussef, Reda, and me, we'd naively imagined we'd be dining out in Spain, no less. "'A feast of tapas in the heart of Algeciras, washed down with sangria! That's the way to celebrate your new life!" Those were the words of Morad, who hadn't spared the superlatives when it came to the food abroad, to the infinite variety of dishes we would find:

fruits that melted in the mouth, unheard of in Moorish lands, every kind of vegetable, no matter what the season, and unbelievably tender, succulent cuts of meat.

Morad knew what he was talking about because he'd lived in Paris for ten years. Ten long, happy years. Paris the beautiful! Paris the mysterious! Paris that to our Bedouin ears sounded like the promise of paradise! Morad had been thrown out three times, so that at the Café France—general headquarters for any would-be immigrant—he'd been awarded the noble title of European Deportee. A richly deserved honorific we were all obliged to use, otherwise he'd lose his temper.

"Morad the European Deportee!" he'd shout. "Yes, sir, say it loud and savor every single syllable! Deported three times, from France and from Europe!"

Morad was as attached to the prestige of his title as he was to the little mother-of-pearl hash pipe that we all coveted. He'd demand this proud honor loud and clear as his due, like the one bestowed on pilgrims back from Mecca. We were fascinated by all his different stories, his fabulous escapades and amorous exploits. He could count on bringing a hush to the table whenever he talked about France, especially Paris, and the swanky restaurant on rue Mazarine where he'd worked for years: "Chez Albert, Portuguese Specialties" the neon sign flashed. The kitchen gave on to a small backyard where his "bachelor pad" was tucked away on the ground floor. A charming studio apartment—or *studette* as they elegantly term it in the capital—with every mod con: a comfy little bed, a red pine wardrobe, a color TV, an electric stove on top of the fridge, an earthenware basin, and a shower with a zip-up plastic curtain. And all that in the space of six square meters—incredible. Two meters by three, do I hear any advance on that? But what does any of it matter? It was there, within those walls covered in flowery paper, under that cracked ceiling with its bare bulb, by that small half-blocked-up basement window, yes, that was where his most cherished memories resided.

Memories that were as illicit as he was—Momo, Chez Albert's little fuzzhead. In the beginning, he'd done eleven hours a day washing up in a smoke-filled kitchen that reeked of cod, a never-ending round of plates, glasses, and cutlery. Morad never complained; on the contrary, he was always up to the job, his enthusiasm equalled only by his roaring laughter and playful spirit, ever ready to offer a helping hand to Garcia, the obese vegetable-peeler whose fingers swelled up in the damp. Then he'd be sweeping up over here, wiping down over there. Occasionally he'd peek through the serving hatch at the merry, booming dining room, where, choking with laughter or overcome by fits of melancholy, drunk on *vinho verde*, men and women of every stamp were devoting all their energy to living life to the fullest.

Morad used to say to himself that one day, maybe, his turn would come to serve on the restaurant floor—like Benoit, that French moron who grumbled all night long, totally oblivious to how privileged he was. They were simple blessings, true, but genuine ones: to see the customers close up, smile at them, talk to them as an equal, recommend dishes that he, Momo, Chez Albert's little fuzzhead, knew down to the last herb. Then, if it so happened he felt like chatting, he could have told them about Morocco. He knew it like the back of his hand, from the Sahara to Tetouan, imperial cities and all. He could still remember the odd bits of history he used to churn out for the tourists, from when he'd passed himself off as a guide in Marrakesh. Yes, one day, maybe . . .

Garcia was an Andalusian from Almería—a cousin, then. He'd been working at the restaurant since it opened, ten years before Momo's arrival, which probably explained the hundred kilos of fat that covered his bones, which he had more and more trouble dragging from one chair to another. Despite his yellow teeth and premature balding, Garcia wasn't bad-looking; his features, though swamped by bloated cheeks, retained a certain grace. His neck was almost nonexistent; sunk into his shoulders, it unfurled in a triple chin, which gave him the leisurely, majestic self-importance of a turkey. Momo would stroke him on the head every time he passed by. Which drove Garcia mad. The moment he started to mumble curses in Spanish the whole kitchen would burst out laughing. He'd let rip, spluttering a string of filthy insults before dissolving into laughter himself. Oh, he was a lovely man, Garcia Gomez, everyone liked him. The waiters never failed to set aside the best bits of almond cake for him, or the ice cream with chantilly that the sated diners barely touched. From time to time the cook, too, sent him a plate of this or that to make his mouth water. He did so love a good feed, Garcia Gomez! Anyway, besides peeling vegetables and sleeping, that was all he did in life. And it made him happy.

On Saturdays, at the end of the shift, Momo would make it his job to wash the red convertible that belonged to the manager, Mr. José. It would look good, he thought. He'd polish it with such care that the big boss, who was crazy about old cars, would publicly favor him with pats on the back. Momo was so proud! His joy would reach its peak when Mr. José tossed him a packet of cigarettes over the counter—real American ones with golden filters—which he'd catch in mid-air and proceed in grand style to offer round to everyone.

Come midnight, when all the customers had left and all the tables were laid, everyone would relax. The kitchen staff would come out to hear all the goings-on in the dining room; there were always a few that were good for a laugh. Jokes and hilarity blew away the stress of the evening, and then even Benoit would seem almost likeable. After the barman had bought a round, it was the boss's turn, and two or three glasses of the bitter almond liqueur would give Momo the courage to stick his nose out of doors.

Ah, how good it felt to breathe the fresh air of rue Mazarine! He'd set off for a stroll as far as place de l'Odéon, which day and night was always packed. He'd wander past the bright windows of the shops and the cafés, the brasseries with their gleaming zinc bars, the art galleries filled with bizarre objects, the bookshops for insomniacs. He'd scan the giant cinema posters, on the lookout for an Indian or a karate film, both pretty rare commodities in the Latin Quarter. Weather permitting, he'd sit at the foot of the statue of Danton, not far from the mouth of the metro, and admire the blonde creatures spilled out in waves by the moving staircase.

"An *escalator*," he explained. "An escalator!" we'd all repeat in unison. The word had a tang of conquest, and seeing the pleasingly lofty look in the eyes of the European Deportee, our own eyes—of would-be immigrants, anonymous conquistadors—would light up in turn. He'd pause significantly, as if to give us time to fully digest our dreams.

A toke of hash, a gulp of tea, and he'd be back to strolling the cobbled alleys of the capital city. Morad had developed something of a sixth sense there, a surefire method of detecting cops, riot police, officers, immigration, or anyone in uniform. He'd be the first to spot even a harmless postman in a radius of three hundred meters. Better still, he'd honed this instinct so that he could unmask private detectives or even plainclothes police. Which wasn't that hard, in fact, since they'd be strutting about like film stars, trying to outmacho each other in their regulation costume of faded jeans, beat-up leather jackets, designer stubble, Ray-Bans, and that tough-guy look that made him laugh and tremble at the same time.

The truth was Morad rarely strayed far from the restaurant. He was happy just walking around the area, up and down those streets with their magical names: Seine, Buci, Bonaparte, Monsieur-le-Prince, l'Ancienne Comédie. If the alcohol led him farther afield, where the cabarets, jazz, and cocktail bars thrived, the cafés for intellectuals and underground dance clubs, the whole fascinating stage set for the beautiful people, he'd be twice as vigilant. In case of any bother, or even a hint of bother, he could run back to his lonely kingdom, his cold bed and his glossy paper goddesses cut out of *Playboy*. There he'd watch television late into the night, because he didn't like sleeping. Because he didn't like dreaming. Because there was a dream that haunted his sleep, that came back to torment his nights too often, that pursued him like a macabre episode of some Brazilian soap opera. A dream that didn't bode well—he, Momo, Chez Albert's little fuzzhead, had no doubt about that.

4

A SALTY GUST of wind shook us. Reda woke with a start. I put my hand on his head and told him to go back to sleep.

He looked up and said, "I'm hungry."

"Me too," I replied.

"I'm cold."

"Go back to sleep then! It's the best way to escape."

Kacem Judi surprised us by taking three superb navel oranges from his bag and offering them round without asking anything in return—at least not immediately. While I wavered, Reda and Yussef pounced and set about peeling them. We hadn't eaten since last night's broad beans, a delicious purée with olive oil and just the right amount of chili, which I'd stuffed myself with, afraid I wouldn't eat them again in a long time, or maybe ever. We'd eaten so much that at dawn, when we left town, we'd only had coffee, and that was it. So those oranges were worth their weight in gold; had he asked me for a thousand pesetas

I'd have unpicked the hem of my belt straight away and handed them over.

In the month we'd spent in Tangier, waiting to leave, I'd become convinced that men only give something in order to get back more. But even I had to admit that the Algerian's offer looked like pure generosity. Or maybe pity, because everything about Reda aroused pity: his clumsiness, his endless whining, his floppy body, his gummed-up eye-lashes—everything, absolutely everything. I was ashamed of him. But what can you do, you don't choose *your blood*. He'd always borne bad luck deep in his gut; like the stone in the fruit, they grew together.

After my aunt's suicide, his twin brother and he had ended up caught in my grandmother's snare. Grandma was a real menace, worse than any stepmother. Their father, a small-time poultry farmer, had married a little fourteen-year-old savage as soon as the mourning period ended, and had more or less forgotten them. Where we come from, sui-cide is still very rare; it occurs to us less, the more actual reasons we have to do it—to be rid, once and for all, of the grinding worry, the hardship, the blood-sucking local authorities, to make a clean break, like waving a magic wand, bringing a curtain down on our misery. No, pride is more developed with us than elsewhere, our country-men prefer to die little by little, from hard wear and grief. In France, for example, it's very different; according to Morad, they have a perfectly respectable suicide rate. In the North, the better your life is, the more you want to blow your brains out! That said, the situation isn't entirely hopeless: since we're one revolution behind the West, we're bound to catch up with their statistics one of these days.

So anyway, my aunt's suicide was the major event of the season; in the village, it was all they talked about. The fact that it was so unusual made this seemingly level-headed woman's tragedy all the more dreadful. To this day, people wonder how a simple reply could have provoked such an appalling death.

Reda wasn't yet five years old, that Friday in July when he dragged his twin brother down to the bottom of the yard, to the henhouse. It was the first time they'd climbed over the wire netting. Not far away, their mother was quietly going about the housework; the pot was simmering on the brazier, their father would soon be home. The two children had begun playing with the chicks, shouting as they ran after them. In a game of trying to put them to sleep, they had snapped the necks of about twenty, as the crazed hens looked on, cackling and knocking against the wire. Then they plucked them carefully until they were bald and piled the little bodies in a hole, the way adults do during epidemics or war, except that instead of tipping earth over them, they covered the creatures with their own feathers. So they'd be all nice and warm, they thought. After a while, they started picking up handfuls from the mound of little yellow feathers and throwing them high in the cage, running squealing under the silken rain that fell on their curly hair and brown skin and stuck to their woollen djellabas.

Their mother caught them hunting a dozen survivors in a cloud of dust. Seeing her meager capital on the verge of complete collapse, she flew at them and grabbed his twin brother, while Reda ran off as fast as his legs would carry him. She pulled off one of her slippers and with all her strength gave those murderous hands a memorable beating. By the time she caught up with Reda, her rage was blunted and his punishment much less severe.

This episode might have remained a harmless family incident had the twin's hands not swollen up badly that same evening. Complaining of terrible pain, the boy couldn't sleep all night. First thing next morning, his mother marched him off to the barber's, who took one look and diagnosed multiple fractures. Then he rolled up his sleeves, put on his bifocals, and immediately started work. He tugged on each finger to realign the bones, massaged the tiny hands and set them with bamboo sticks, bandaged them firmly, and with a couple of slaps revived the boy, who had fainted in the meantime.

Once again, things might have been left there and everything would have returned to normal. But alas, fate decided otherwise. A life suddenly collapses and existences are turned upside down, and no one can do a thing about it.

Tears may not solve anything, but they always bring relief. Their mother shed plenty during those days. The twin's bandages stayed on for two weeks, all of which he spent squirming with pain and complaining of awful itching. When they consulted the barber again, he was reassuring, explaining that the bones were most likely on the mend or knitting together, and the main thing was not to worry. The mother wasn't having that; out of patience, she decided to trust to instinct alone and unrolled the little one's bandages. Then the full horror greeted her. The hands, turned a bluish color, hadn't gone down at all; they were actually losing their skin, and suppurating abscesses were spreading here and there, giving off a putrid smell. The bamboo had become embedded in the flesh and was sticking to the whitish bones, which were showing through in places. When she pulled the splints out, the mother nearly fainted. She took a deep breath and composed herself, then she put on her djellaba, settled her two children astride the she-ass and hurriedly left the village, heading for the main road.

She found her husband in the shade of a giant plane tree where he often lay down for a rest, a mass of chickens tied by the feet in bunches around him. Before he could even show his surprise, she burst into tears, displaying the little boy's tortured hands. The father examined them closely and frowned, which meant that he thought a visit to the pharmacy was inevitable, urgent even. He didn't like the pharmacist, or that rogue of a nurse who'd fleece you for even an aspirin. But the state of the boy's hands, not to mention the wrath in his mother's eyes, forbade prevarication. Reluctantly, he opened his pouch, groped around, and pulled out a grimy note from a whole wad secured with an elastic band, as if he were peeling off his own skin, and handed it over. The mother slipped it into her blouse, dealt the ass a blow, and set off for the pharmacy.

It was a hot day, without a breath of air to ease the journey. Letting himself be gently rocked by the donkey, Reda
held his brother round the waist and smiled at his mother
whenever their eyes met. Of the two boys, he knew that he
was her favorite. The mother walked in silence, sometimes
on the shoulder and sometimes on the asphalt, which infuri-
ated the lorry drivers, whose hysterical hooting frightened
the children. They crossed the Tassaout riverbed, dried out
in the blazing heat, its banks still flecked with green, as if
living off the memory of the water they'd once bordered.
Seeing the brick building in the distance, the mother quick-
ened her pace. All the fatigue of the journey, which had
lasted three hours, fell away at the sight of the nurse's white
tunic, who was sitting on a bench by the door, reading a
paper. He glanced up at the visitors and then went back to
his paper. The mother went over and as she greeted him, discreetly slipped him the note, still warm from her bosom. The
effect was instantaneous: the slab-cheeked man stood up, all
smiles, went over to the children and even took the trouble
to lift them down from the ass and carry them inside.

A huge tiled room, with an operating table in the middle
that must once have been white. A glass dresser containing
mercurochrome and methylated spirits, and a big sack of aspirin tablets, probably foreign aid. The nurse put the sick child
down on the table, slowly undid his bandages, and recoiled
in disgust, making the already charged atmosphere still more
oppressive. The child's injuries looked nasty. He didn't want
to appear alarmist or talk of catastrophe, but what he saw

there was not very heartening. He avoided the word gangrene, but seemed to be thinking it intently. He would only disinfect the wounds and carefully dress them. The kid must be taken to hospital urgently, which, in that godforsaken place, wasn't so simple. The ambulance only came by once a day, in the early morning, and on donkey's back it would take at least a week. And yet what worried the mother the most, what truly alerted her to the gravity of the situation, was not the nurse's words, or his awkwardness, but the fact that without the least hesitation he gave her back her crumpled old note.

That was unheard of. She shook her head. He insisted, as if he'd sensed some curse on the money, the whiff of a widow and orphan. Now the mother had no idea what to do. She picked up the injured child, set him on her back, settled her other boy on the ass and prepared to leave. She stared hard into the nurse's averted eyes.

"Your ambulance mustn't leave without my son, sir. His father will bring him back tomorrow, at dawn."

He nodded, smiling. The mother took off her slippers— the very ones that had crushed her little one's hands—and flung them as far as she could, into the thistles. Broken-hearted, she walked barefoot back to the village.

The tragedy occurred a month later, in the blistering heat of August. Since the boy had come back with both hands amputated, his mother hadn't spoken. She didn't cry, she didn't complain, she just got on with the cooking and housework as usual. Sometimes she'd stop to look through the curtains at the children playing on the patio, the way she used to do. The boy's fingers still hurt a little—an absurd sensation, since they were under the ground somewhere. Nevertheless, he felt them. Although he'd soon understood and accepted his handicap, his body refused to admit its mutilation. At mealtimes, his mother would take him on her knee and feed him affectionately. She would have so loved to breathe sweet words in his ear, comforting words, like in the old days, but she couldn't. They stayed buried in the pit of her stomach, refusing to obey, or at best just evaporating in useless sighs. Only the odd vague smile could express her tenderness, but they were melancholy smiles, stretched thin to stifle her sobs. She'd stroke his hair and cover him in kisses. Suddenly relegated to second place, Reda didn't think much of all this new, ardent attention bestowed on his brother, who, as far as he could see, was as cheerful as ever. As for their father, he took so little part in family life that he didn't seem too upset by events.

One morning, the boy came to join his mother in the kitchen. Making no sound, he sat down on a stool in a dark corner and watched her blowing on the fire, her face and hands flushed from the heat of the embers as she bent over the hearth. Unaware of the child's presence, she diligently carried on with her work, as if she hadn't a care in the world, preparing the semolina wheat biscuits the little ones adored.

"That smells good!" he said.

She gave a start, turned round and smiled at him. A moment later, she spoke to him for the first time.

"Would you like one?"

He ran to her, overjoyed to hear her voice, put his stumps together and managed to catch the biscuit.

"Look, Mom! I can do it all by myself!"

She looked down. A tear ran down her cheek.

"Why are you crying, Mommy?"

She didn't answer.

"I don't want you to cry! I'll never do anything naughty again, Mommy, I promise! Look, even if I wanted to I wouldn't be able to now . . ."

The mother's face abruptly changed. Pale, her eyes empty, she stood up slowly and left the kitchen as if she were sleepwalking. She went out into the yard, flooded with light, where Reda was having fun making a terrible racket, dragging a sardine tin along on a string. She didn't look round as she passed him but walked along by the henhouse, brushing her emaciated hands against the wire netting. She then climbed up on the coping, undid her long tress of hair—an act that remains unexplained to this day—and let herself fall like a stone into the well.

The mother can't have died straight away, although Reda's memory was rather vague about that. It also should be said that no one really dared ask him any details, because his voice would start to shake and his eyes fill with tears. But it is known that when the two children, panic-stricken, ran to the well, they thought they heard something like a sigh, a murmur rising from the belly of the earth. It was their mother asking forgiveness.

5

BENEATH THE UPTURNED boat there reigned a peace that Nuara and her baby wouldn't have exchanged for anything in the world. Of course it was cramped, but there was enough space to do simple things, like opening the bag she'd made sure not to leave outside, changing the baby's diapers, giving him the breast again, and eating herself—because sea air makes you so ravenous! More than once she banged into the tiller in the middle. And then she almost laughed, wondering what on earth she was doing under there in the middle of the night, in that tomblike darkness, so far from her home and family, surrounded by this gang of strapping men she barely knew. Did she have the right to inflict this hardship on her baby? She didn't know. All she could think of was Suleiman, her hero, her sun, her husband and master. It had been a year now since the last news from him—no letter, no money order, nothing. Not even one of the telephone calls she usually had on holidays.

Nuara used to look forward to them so impatiently! She was always waiting for the moment when the young Berber in overalls with the shaved head would come and knock at her door, loudly announcing, "A call from France! From France! Mr. Suleiman will be calling the general store again in a quarter of an hour!"

Nuara's heart would go wild in her little breast. She'd put on her slippers, wrap herself in her haik, and run over to one-eyed Ahmad's, the only shopkeeper in the area who had a phone. He was a real bloodsucker, he even made you pay for incoming calls! But what did it matter, nothing was too much for Suleiman—her cousin, her friend, her gentle husband, this man who was her whole life.

Even as a child, mothers, aunts, and sisters had all impressed on her the fact that she was pledged to him, that she would belong to him always, body and soul, that she owed him respect and obedience. But even if no one had expected anything of her, she would have pledged herself to him. Because he was handsome, Suleiman, because such tenderness, light, and promise flowed from his big, dark eyes. Because, when he and his friends were playing card games with Spanish cards, his irresistible laugh would fill the whole house with joy, and her heart with it. Because, when he sensed she was sad, that a heavy sorrow was weighing on her, he'd come to her slowly, enfold her in his loving gaze, cup her face in his big-veined hands, and whisper in her ear things that made her laugh out loud, even as the tears clouded her eyes.

He was all that, Suleiman, and more besides. Once a year, he'd come back from France, his bags crammed with presents: silky satin material for caftans, flannel and mohair for djellabas, richly brocaded scarves, stopwatches, sunglasses, electric torches, T-shirts, jumpers, cooking utensils, and an infinite variety of objects no one knew how to use but that looked precious. Lalla Maryam, Nuara's mother-in-law and aunt, would pack them away in the cupboard, saying they were sure to use them one day. Then the whole family would come out to welcome him. He'd have a little something for each of them, and not forget anyone, not even Tamu, the little black girl the household had acquired.

Suleiman liked this girl, Nuara did too: she treated her like a younger sister. She pitied her, really. There'd been no sign of life from her father since he'd brought her down from the mountains, a thin, sickly thing. He was afraid she wouldn't last long working in one of the houses in the medina, because he knew how much she could eat. Touched by her sparkling eyes and dimpled smile, Lalla Maryam had agreed to take her on. The father asked nothing in return, just that his little ten-year-old would not go hungry. He had a whole brood up there in his village—eight, to be exact, not counting the three that died young—and nothing to feed them with. After he'd left, Tamu had started guzzling anything she could get her hands on, as if she were discovering food for the first time in her life. Dried fruit, raw vegetables, granulated sugar, even flour, which she stuffed down by the spoonful. When she cleaned up after a meal, you could have sworn a cloud of locusts had passed through. She licked the plates, gnawed on the bones, polished off crusts that would normally be left out for the birds. Eventually, the cat had left the house in despair.

Lalla Maryam would have got rid of her as soon as possible if her peasant of a father had left an address. They'd waited until the end of the month. Then the next month. Nothing, no news. Like it or not, they'd kept her. You couldn't say Tamu had exactly improved with time—she went on eating enough for four—but you had to admit that she worked at least as hard; in that sense, she paid her way. In the space of only a year, she'd succeeded in making herself part of the household—indispensable, even. Waiting on everyone hand and foot, she was always on the go, busying herself with the housework and the washing, never standing still. She learned to cook by watching her mistress. She'd sit next to her peeling vegetables, chopping parsley and coriander, gutting and cleaning chickens, washing pots, plates, knives—all the jobs that apprentices usually do. One day, when Lalla Maryam was ill, Tamu seized her chance to make the meal: a cardoon tagine with bitter olives, no less. The result had surprised everyone, it was utterly delicious—compliments all round. From then on, she'd been put in charge of the stoves and ruled expertly over the kitchen. She'd be at market from first light, haggling until it came to tears, not giving in until she came back with as many supplies as possible. As Lalla Maryam began to grow old, she'd thank heaven morning and night for sending her such a pearl.

The previous summer, when Suleiman's car had pulled up at the door, it was Tamu who'd proclaimed the news, "It's Uncle Sulei! Uncle Sulei's here!"

Dressed in her old, crumpled housecoat, her heart thudding, no makeup, Nuara had rushed barefoot to the door. Having replayed their reunion over and over in her mind's eye, didn't it just serve her right! In her head, of course, it had all gone according to the rules: she'd imagined herself standing in the doorway, fresh-faced and bright-eyed, resplendent in her gold-embroidered caftan, her hair down, holding a tray of stuffed dates in hands colored with henna, and Tamu by her side carrying the carafe of milk scented with orange blossom. But no, he'd gone and spoiled it all by just turning up out of the blue like that. Still, who cared: there he was, smiling radiantly in spite of his tiredness. She stared at him in bewilderment, like a rag and bone girl before a prince. He went to her and gathered her in his arms, squeezing her tight. He was so big! Nuara wept quietly. She blamed herself for not being beautiful, for being nothing like a princess.

Then the whole tribe was let loose: aunts, sisters-in-law, cousins, neighbors . . . In a flash the patio was black with people. Everyone came out to admire the white, metallic *station wagon* that was stuffed to bursting and had an enormous refrigerator tied on the roof rack. In the uproar, Suleiman and Nuara constantly caught each other's eye.

Then she'd joined the clan of women in the kitchen and Suleiman had let himself be dragged off by the men to the sitting room; he had no end of fabulous stories to tell.

When night fell, they were reunited in their room, high up on the terrace. The bed was set back in an alcove lit by candles, piled with cushions she'd embroidered herself. They fell upon it and made love until dawn. Suleiman was as insatiable for love as Tamu was for food, it was as if he were making up for the eleven months of abstinence—or so he'd have her believe. Either way, Nuara welcomed a real lion into her arms that night.

The days passed quickly. Sometimes Suleiman would suggest a drive into town in his beautiful white car. She was so proud. Aunts, sisters-in-law, and neighbors would all stand at their windows to watch them go by: she in her flower print djellaba, without a veil, and he in an impeccably ironed double-breasted suit, his black shoes gleaming. They'd go for a walk under the olive trees of the Menara, or to the Agdal park. She so loved the lakes in the Agdal, especially the one where a great king had once drowned. There was such a pretty view: on one side, beyond the olive grove, palms stretching into the distance, motionless, tantalizing; on the other, the snow-clad, regal peaks of the Atlas mountains. The dead king had a particular fondness for this spot. Surrounded by his retinue, he'd often be rowed out in his royal boat to the middle of the lake and stay there for hours, mulling over the nation's affairs, stimulated by the coolness and fairy tale beauty of the place. Like Nuara, he must have been susceptible to sunsets. As one spring afternoon was drawing to a close, in circumstances some thought suspicious, his boat had capsized. He and his retinue had instantly perished, trapped in the forest of seaweed that slept below. Only one young slave, probably from a village on the banks, had just about made it to shore. But it was no use; he was beheaded as soon as he'd been fished out.

He should have saved his master first, thought Nuara. Still, the king wasn't young anymore. Perhaps losing your life in such a beautiful way was really a royal death, an end in keeping with the grandeur of his reign—to reach the sky by sinking into its reflection, in a placid lake suspended between date palms and everlasting snows. Of any death, wasn't this the one she herself would have desired, given the choice? Preferably at the magical sunset hour, when birds are flitting back to their nests and the chorus of the muezzin fills the glowing firmament. She was sure that when the time came she wouldn't object to such an end.

Under the boat, the oxygen must have been running low. Nuara had dug a little tunnel toward the outside world, but the wind kept on blocking it with sand and from time to time we'd see a hand coming out of the ground like a zombie's. At first we'd been terrified, because the mother and baby had completely slipped our minds, but then it made us laugh, especially when Pafadnam teasingly pinched her thumb. Nuara screamed so loud the baby woke up. She must have thought she'd been bitten by a crab. Even Kacem Judi, who was having trouble concealing his attraction to her, had smiled. After that, the hand hadn't reappeared; Nuara stayed under the boat, silent and wary, like a tortoise under its shell.

She'd told us her story in detail, one afternoon in the Café France. As usual, we were at the table at the back, minds numbed by kif and heat, clustered around our idol, the European Deportee. Nuara was the only woman in the café; the child she held in her lap stopped people from talking. Whatever the cost, she wanted to join Suleiman in France. In Poissy, to be precise. She showed us his address on a bit of paper that was so crumpled it was hard to make it out. He was living in a hostel for guest workers, next to some main road or other. She said that the reason he hadn't sent news all this time was because something bad had happened. She was convinced of it. She suspected her mother-in-law hadn't told her the truth. They must have known, but they wouldn't have wanted to tell her because she was heavily pregnant; she was already in her eighth month. Suleiman didn't know. She'd caught the family whispering plenty of times, and exchanging knowing looks over her head. She pretended not to notice, but it hurt her, like the awkward silences or sudden stiffness her presence caused in the household.

One evening, she'd burst into tears in Tamu's arms. The girl had tried to console her, maintaining that no one knew a thing about Uncle Sulei, and there was no way any news could have escaped her, Tamu, who listened in on everything. But it was true Lalla Maryam had serious money worries, probably because Uncle Sulei didn't send his money orders anymore. She was intending to sell the refrigerator to one-eyed Ahmad; they only used it for storage in any case, since the neighborhood still hadn't got electricity.

That night, Tamu had slept in Nuara's bed. They'd talked and talked, about everything and nothing—about how alone they each felt. Tamu had confided that one of these days she'd love to go back home to the mountains. Her brothers and sisters must have grown up; she missed them. She said she wasn't sure she could remember her mother's face, as if every day time made it fade a little more. She said she was happy to have found a family and especially to have her, Nuara, as a sister and confidante, that she wouldn't leave her for anything in the world. When Uncle Suleiman came back for good and bought a house in the new part of town, which was what he wanted, a beautiful big house with tiles, running water, and electric light, she'd come and live with them like a shot. She'd take care of everything, the shopping, the cooking, the housework. In the daytime she'd carry the baby on her back, as if it were her own. Had she chosen a first name yet? If it was a boy, Sufyan would be wonderful. Nuara wouldn't have to worry about a thing; she could rest, or go walking with her man in the Agdal park, by the lake of the drowned king. But she should go to sleep now and stop brooding on her sadness, because the baby she was carrying was so close to her heart that it could see everything that went on there.

Tamu had stretched out beside her sister, put her hand on her belly, and closed her eyes. Under her slender fingers, she had felt the baby wriggle; it was still awake.

6

WE'D SPEND WHOLE days sitting around Momo in the Café France, in a dream, smoking pipe after pipe of hash, rolling joints whenever a cigarette with good tobacco came our way, sipping sweet mint tea and bursting into fits of helpless laughter over nothing, casually watching as people and time passed by. ~~You could fritter your life away unawares on that busy but peaceful square, in that artificial bliss and tranquillity~~. The hippies sitting beside us, not realizing their day was long gone, continued to fade away without even caring. They were old before their time, not because it was their fate, like us, but because they'd chosen to burn the candle at both ends.

What a waste, don't you think, all those red, blue, green, and maroon passports moldering in the pockets of all those ripped jeans. Ah, now if I'd had one, I'd have taken care of it, I'd have cosseted it, pressed it to my heart, I'd have hidden it somewhere the thieving and envious wouldn't ever be able to find it, sewn it into my own skin, right in the middle of my chest, so I'd only have to unbutton my shirt to show it when I was crossing borders. What were they after, these foreigners, poking around in our poverty? What did they want from us, these people who taunted us with their freedom to come and go as they pleased? I'd have happily changed places with the most pathetic of them all. Just think! To be able to leave, leave and forget this devouring sun, this lethargy and idleness, this corruption and filth, the cowardice and deceit that are our lot here.

When I'd get angry, Yussef's big, credulous eyes would open even wider. I think he was ready to sew anything into his skin as well if it'd get him through Immigration. That boy's story was one of the strangest I'd heard; Momo had told it to us one night in the café, first making us promise to keep it to ourselves and not breathe a word to anyone. He had been sworn to secrecy himself by the man who'd introduced them a month earlier. That's because in our country we're very suspicious of anyone who's suffered terrible misfortune; we shrink from them, they're never welcome anywhere, because a curse is contagious like scabies, everyone knows that.

Tall and thin, with a gentle, loyal expression in his eyes, Yussef was the eldest of five children. There were three girls, of eight, ten, and twelve, and a boy of six who, although he was mute, kicked up one hell of a din all day long. In the mornings Yussef worked in the souk making leather slippers and in the afternoons at a bazaar where he sold kitchenware made of copper, tin, camel bone, and thuja root. Half of his income went to his family; it didn't amount to much but it helped them get by at the end of the month, often the hardest time.

A repo man by profession and an influential figure in the neighborhood, his father took care of all sorts of odd jobs at the town hall: cleaning, running errands to the shops, mediating between corrupt civil servants and people desperate for their papers, constantly to-ing and fro-ing between the corner café and various offices, washing officials' cars, informing for the police—a whole range of minor activities that made the time pass quickly. He and his family occupied the ground floor of a house that they shared with other tenants, and his two wives lived together in perfect harmony—no, more than that, they shared a real affection, a complicity that many found hard to comprehend.

Once a week, the two wives would go to the Moorish baths together. They'd do their shopping hand in hand, automatically agreeing on which patterns to choose, what brocaded scarf or billowing dress. One wife's purse belonged to the other. There were never any fallings out, never a raised voice. If there was a misunderstanding, they'd sit down with a pot of tea, talk the matter over as calmly as could be, and soon smooth out any difference of opinion. You couldn't invite one anywhere without the other. At weddings or circumcisions, they'd sit side by side, chatting and giggling under their headscarves, criticizing as one a caftan they thought gaudy or too revealing, kohl applied too thickly or dragged all the way to the ear; a newcomer's simpering, or a young thing's clumsy attempts to charm the mother of an unmarried man, and a thousand other juicy details that never went unremarked. If something eluded one, the other was sure to pick up on it. They really were a sight, these two, planted on their majestic rumps, pursing their lips like schoolgirls who've got the giggles and are trying to stop, in case they'll be punished. Unable to have children of her own, the first wife helped bring up those of the second wife, so much so that they called their step-mother Mommy and their real mother Lalla.

The father was none too pleased with this state of affairs; it worried him, his wives being this close. He'd tried in the past to make trouble between them, but the two women had stood shoulder to shoulder, unmoved by his provocations. Occasionally he'd dangle the specter of a third marriage before them, a fresh, pretty young tigress who'd immediately become mistress of the household. The threat unnerved them but they didn't show it. Out of sight, they'd concoct magical infusions that they made him take every day; they'd spy on him and go through his pockets, sift the rumors that malicious gossips never failed to report, and then take the appropriate action.

Apart from that, everything in the household was going smoothly; there was an unmistakable air of peace and tranquillity. Lalla and the mother had two rooms each, with a patio between them where they spent most of their time, chatting, laughing, and gossiping away from dusk till dawn. As they grew older, they became even closer, to the extent that it would never have occurred to Lalla, who suffered from terrible rheumatism, not to share her medicine with her companion, even though she was in perfect health. The doctor was at his wits' end; he pointed out that there were grave risks, but it wasn't any use, he couldn't make them listen. They'd carry on in secret: it was one pill for you, one pill for me; three drops for you, three drops for me.

"What's good for me couldn't possibly hurt you!"

You try telling them different.

Perched on his old black bicycle with the handlebars raised like a bull's horns, his fez proudly outlined against the sky, the father would ride back and forth through the souk four times a day. He was respected and feared in equal measure, because everyone in the neighborhood knew he had the ear of his superiors. Some even claimed he had access to the governor in person. Give him his cut and he could get you a birth certificate within two weeks and a passport in less than three months. It wouldn't much matter if a document was missing; with a wallet next to your heart, you can always come to an arrangement. So, on the face of it, the man wasn't hard up. Why the devil then did he go and steal that sack of corn from the town hall basement? Admittedly, his salary wasn't enough to feed his family, but he had other sources of income here and there, even gifts in kind sometimes. No, Satan must have been there that night, in that huge damp cellar, piled high with bulging sacks.

There were so many of them that no one would notice if one went missing; the father made his decision quickly. The sack was heavy, the fear of being caught gave him the strength of ten, and he hoisted it up in one go. He went down a long dark corridor, through a first door, then a second, up some stairs and through a gate he had the key for, and then retrieved his bicycle, which was leaning against a eucalyptus tree. The nightwatchman didn't see a thing, nor did the people sitting on the low wall surrounding the park. Wedging the sack between the saddle and handlebars, the father made straight for his house. It was almost dark and the souk was full of people. Ducking down the alleyways through the crowds, past the dimly lit shops, cafés, and stalls, lowering his head to avoid seeing anyone he knew, he eventually arrived home, where his wives gave him a warm welcome. The grain was superb and the corn was clean, no stones or insects; there was no need to wash it, and Yussef would take it to the mill the next day.

It had all begun with that wretched theft.

It was an afternoon in late spring, just before the vicious heat that mired people deep in torpor all summer long. Yussef's father wasn't hungry that day; he had an upset stomach, so he ate some melon rather than the usual tagine of chickpeas and artichoke hearts. Coming back through the square, Yussef hadn't been able to resist the enticing smell of grilled meat—he put away a hearty sausage sandwich, with plenty of chili. At home his mother, Lalla, the children, their neighbor, and her cousin, who'd come to spend the holiday in Marrakesh, had all sat down to a mouthwatering feast. The bread was still hot from the oven. Yussef and his father just took tea in the front room, bending over the transistor radio to catch the one o'clock news. In a dry, solemn voice, the broadcaster spouted a continuous stream of information, oddly similar to yesterday's, the day's before, and the days' before that. There were details of prestigious visits to the Palace, messages of congratulation received by the Palace or sent by the Palace, monuments unveiled amid great pomp, stones laid for new social amenities that would remain small heaps of cement on patches of waste ground forever. Then came the international news: Palestine and Iraq to keep the fire ablaze in people's hearts, ethnic conflicts and famine in sub-Saharan Africa to make them shudder, a few floods, the occasional spicy death served up with a different garnish, then the football results, the lottery, the weather, and we'd come full circle. At the end of the bulletin, you couldn't help thinking that after all, on balance, life here wasn't so bad; people were wrong to spend all their time complaining. There probably was a better life to be had elsewhere, but there was a lot worse as well.

The silence in the house had suddenly struck Yussef when he stood up to fetch a glass of water for his father. As he went into the living room, at first he thought it was a joke, that everyone had decided for some reason to play dead. His mute brother was by the window, his body convulsing, hands flailing, blue in the face. Yussef went up to

Lalla and his mother; they were playing the game too—a ghoulish game, which was meant to scare him, filling him with a terror that was already making him stagger, there in the middle of the room. Their heads, in matching head-scarves, lay on the table, their faces spotted with foam, their eyes rolled upward, while the cat went on calmly eating the stew, its paws in the still-warm plate.

Yussef began to howl like someone possessed, then, taking his brother in his arms, he ran out onto the patio. The upstairs neighbors were leaning out of their windows, others were listening outside the door. Hearing the noise, the father hurried to join him and was confronted in turn with the terrible sight. He crouched down with his back to the wall and covered his ageing face with veiny hands, trying to stammer some verses from the Koran. His lips quivered, his heart shrank to a fistful of snow, his knees buckled, his whole body was bruised and numb, as if it had taken a beating. His three daughters had died here, in front of him, both his wives, his mute son, the neighbor, and her cousin who had come for the holiday. He looked at them, stupefied, helpless. Suddenly he stood up and rushed out to the kitchen, seized the sack of flour and started to pour it down the sink, which blocked up at once. But that didn't stop him and he went on spraying the white powder all around him. Then he fell on the floor and rolled in it, furiously banging his fists on the flagstones until he was bleeding, until he was smashing the bones in his hands, as if the pain could ease this grief that tore at his chest.

How could he have known there was rat poison in the corn? How could he have foreseen such a catastrophe? There'd never been such fine grain, so clean, with no grit or weevils. It must have come from abroad. He should have guessed, he should have known, that damned town hall held no secrets from him. Why hadn't he asked about it? His guilty plan . . . he hadn't wanted to arouse suspicion. And this was the result: he had killed everyone.

No, no, it wasn't him, it was the rats. The father proclaimed his innocence loud and clear, calling to witness the neighbors who came running from upstairs, from the street, from all over, and formed an accusing circle around his distress.

A sorry tale was Yussef's.

Back in the village, we don't use poisoned corn to kill rats, we just block up their holes, which gives us peace for a while. But they always come scurrying back and burrow through the adobe. So then we fill in the holes again. It's a sort of guerrilla warfare we've learned to live with.

The old bailiff was confined to an asylum on the Casablanca road. Yussef went to visit him several times but it didn't do much good; his father didn't recognize him anymore. He was much thinner, he was dirty and he smelled bad. He saw rats everywhere; he'd call them every name imaginable, chase after them and spit on them. Sometimes he'd start running in the visiting room, climb up on a table, a chair, a gurney, and scream and scream, his heavily shadowed eyes staring in terror at the invisible swarm.

Yussef soon gave up these visits, which had become unbearable. There was no question of his staying in Marrakesh, there was nothing and no one for him there now. So he had to leave, go somewhere else, far away. Although he'd sold the entire contents of the house after the tragedy—mattresses, carpets, cushions, kitchenware, clothes, jewelry, etc.—he had only managed to raise three-quarters of the fare. Every youngster knows how much that is, they all dream of making that amount one day. But even so, a week later he'd left for the North. It was on the train taking him to Tangier that he met the guy, obviously a crook, who was going to lead him to Momo. We'd seen them turn up one evening at the Café France. Yussef was all embarrassed but he kept smiling, his eyes darting in every direction, as if to spare us from reading his tragedy in them. Moved by his story, the European Deportee had persuaded the trafficker to agree to a discount, and that was how he'd come to be with us, ready to cheat his destiny and try to squeeze a bit of new life out of it, a better one.

7

IN THE DISTANCE, all along the coastline, it looked as if a row of flickering lights was coming toward us—hundreds of oil lamps, rocking in the wind off the open sea.

We couldn't hear Reda's teeth chattering anymore; he was fast asleep. I'd covered him in the maroon woollen burnous my mother had insisted I take with me. (And it had been a godsend, I'd worn it throughout the month we'd spent in that shitty flophouse in the medina.) But Pafadnam, the big Malian, was having some kind of seizure, which worried us, to say the least; up till then, he'd been very calm and quiet. He'd seemed sturdy and resolute, but now he was going berserk and flailing around in the sand, burrowing into it headfirst as if trying to hide, and bellowing like a camel having its throat slit. Back in the café he'd surprised us with his brave talk and his stories of beating up anyone trying to swindle him. Once he'd almost left for dead some crook who tried to pass himself off as a trafficker. Another time a whole gang of them had wrecked the boat of a con man who claimed he'd taken them to Spain when in fact he'd just taken them out on the high seas for three hours before dropping them on a deserted shore near Tetouan. They'd seen through the scam in time, thanks to the call of the muezzin, which rang out by chance at just the right moment; the man had managed to get away, abandoning his boat and the bag with the money that they'd just given him. Yes, this really was that same heroic Pafadnam, author of such great exploits, who was writhing in front of us and sobbing like an overpaid mourner. Drool was oozing from his mouth, his eyes were bloodshot, and his massive black bulk was shaking, sweating, and moaning. I was glad Reda was asleep and didn't have to see it.

Yarcé suggested we slip some keys into his country-man's hand to drive out the djinn that had taken possession of him. But apart from the trafficker, no one had any: what's the good of keys when you're leaving forever? The trafficker refused outright to lend his—too easy to lose in the sand. Kacem Judi, again, was the one who found the words the demon would understand. He bent over Pafadnam, and explained softly that the flashing lights on the beach were the scavengers' oil lamps. An entire village was out there, women, children, and old people too, who'd come to gather the treasure left by a generous tide before the backwash took it away again. They were harmless, these lights winking on the sand, nothing to do with the powerful flashlights of the coastguard. The invisible djinn seemed placated by these words and it abandoned the huge body, escaping through Pafadnam's upturned eyes. Opening its sack full of unfulfilled dreams, it set the Malian's dreams free and, with a flap of its wings, soared off into the misty night.

We felt it fly away, because at that moment a stinging gust of spray froze us to the bone. Pafadnam came to immediately, haggard and confused. He swore he couldn't remember a thing, he just had a feeling of utter emptiness, as if his insides had been scooped out. He had a terrible headache too. We could well believe it. Kacem Judi gave him his water bottle, and we all had a drink without any objection from him.

Pafadnam was pure Soninké, he came from the area round Ségou, a pretty little town on the right bank of the Niger, to the northwest of Bamako. He wasn't truly destitute, like most people hoping to make the crossing. He'd inherited a plot of land where he built a home with his own hands, a charming bamboo hut with a thatched roof, and planted a vegetable garden, fenced by a cactus hedge, that looked full of promise. But since it as good as never rained, he might as well have inherited nothing. His wife and three children had all moved in, but he had enormous trouble feeding them. He'd work in the fields at harvest time, and otherwise he'd roam around, buying and selling all kinds of knick-knacks. If funds were low he'd fall back on salvage work, but in Africa people only throw something away when it's good for absolutely nothing.

So he'd left his family two months earlier, promis-
ing to come back for them when he'd set himself up in
France, preferably somewhere round Mantes-la-Jolie. His
being with us at all was a feat in itself, if not a miracle, as
the guerrilla war still going on there meant the South of
Morocco was almost completely sealed off by minefields.
Tangier was exactly midway between his village in Mali
and his promised land in the Paris suburbs. It had taken
him a month to cross the desert and two borders, and he'd
needed the luck of the gods to dodge the police roadblocks
all along the route. The bus drivers had robbed him blind
for the passage north; the bogus traffickers had taken the
rest. But who cared, he was here now, safe and sound on
the shifting sands of this beach where the demon had just
flown out of his head. His hands had stopped trembling.
The lights at the water's edge were not about to steal away
his dreams or jail him in some dank cell on a nearby island.
Pafadnam was philosophical about the hazards he encountered along the way, he held no grudges, neither against the
good Lord who'd averted His august gaze from him and
his family, nor against the men who'd starved him.

On the day his cousin—a legal immigrant who'd settled
in Mantes-la-Jolie—had sent him the amount he needed to
attempt the adventure, he'd started dancing and clapping
in the middle of the street. He was singing at the top of his
voice and swaying his head, like the Gnawa of Marrakesh.
The passers-by laughed seeing him so happy, and asked,
"What's got into that big lad, why's he clowning around

the square like a lunatic?" But they liked it too, since luckily joy is even more contagious than grief. Pafadnam was shouting to whoever cared to listen that he had his ticket for paradise in his pocket. Nothing and no one could stop him now, no need for visas or a passport anymore; the ten thousand French francs would take care of all that.

A wise old boy, who saw him leaping up and down like a grasshopper, called him over and invited him to sit down on a tree trunk next to him. His bones were almost poking through his tanned skin; he must have given up eating long ago.

"Listen to me, my boy," he said in a fatherly way, "I have some advice for you."

Pafadnam looked with surprise at the old man, who was calmly fanning himself with a palm frond. "In the days when the French were here, they had a nice little saying they were always drumming into us: 'Don't sell the fur before you've killed the bear.' We have a different saying, though the meaning's much the same. We say that each of our dreams is guarded on its right by an angel and on its left by a djinn, and that these two creatures are in perpetual conflict. For a dream to come true, the two of them have to come to an agreement first. When a dream seems to come true too quickly, that means that the djinn has bowed out. Now if it's in such a hurry, there must be a snake in the grass that you have to beware of as if it were the devil himself. So stop all that singing and dancing and keep your celebrations for the day you're finally reunited with your generous cousin in Mantes-la-Jolie. And in the meantime, put away that money, you big donkey, or you'll get it stolen!"

Pafadnam stood up and respectfully kissed the wise man's shoulder before rushing back to his house, where he shut himself away until the morning of his departure.

Pafadnam, Yarcé, Yussef, Reda, and I had all stayed in the same flophouse in Tangier, a hovel with raffia mats on the floor and an indescribable smell of sweat, unwashed feet, kids' piss, cold fried food, animal dung, bad breath, kif, and tobacco mixed with other unidentifiable vile odors. Because it was so cheap, the flophouse attracted the dregs of humanity, a bunch of beggars and pickpockets. At first, Reda had refused to go in. "I'd rather die than spend a single minute in that dump!" he'd shouted. I'd had to use plenty of tact and cast-iron logic to persuade him to follow me. And I hadn't lied to him either; boys who slept out at night did get raped. Reda wasn't pretty or white, he was rather puny and he had a flat ass, but that wouldn't make any difference; there's nothing more dangerous than a rutting male in a dark alley. This argument had sunk in, and we'd entered the hallway where a man in a white gandoura was sitting cross-legged behind a large padlocked box, batting flies away with a doum palm swatter. Other men were playing draughts beside him, noisily sipping viscous tea.

I'd paid up without a fuss. Reda had dragged his feet but eventually he'd come after me. It hadn't been easy finding our friends in that pit; they must have been scrimping on electricity because we could hardly see a thing. A colonnade ran round a manure-strewn courtyard that was used as a stable: donkeys, mules, sheep, and goats jostled for space, tended by half-asleep Bedouin herdsmen. Curled up between bundles and packsaddles, djellabas and burnouses, skinny little girls and boys watched us go by—future servants in big houses, waiters in cheap restaurants, or, in the worst cases, chancing their luck on the streets of Tangier. I thought of little brother, I wouldn't have liked to see him in there. Some of them smiled as we carefully threaded our way to the back. Lying in a corner with their heads propped up on their bags, Yussef and the Malians were waiting for us. They didn't seem bothered by the stench and we got used to it after a few minutes. Worse, we added to it, as Reda stank of sweat and so did I, though not as badly.

Compared to us midgets, Pafadnam was a giant. Everything about him was larger than life. His feet, which I examined under the table, were three times the size of mine, no joke. One day I even saw him take hold of a huge watermelon in one hand. In his honest, gleaming, olive-black face, the first thing you noticed was his solid meat-eater's jaw and rounded cheekbones that hid laughing eyes. He was handsome, Pafadnam, with a wild, virile beauty. You had to wonder how Africa, so impoverished, half-starved, could have sired such a colossus. And yet he was humble and fearful and made himself as small as his gigantic frame allowed. Seeing him with his back bent double, folded in on himself, with the air of someone apologizing for existing, it was obvious he'd already slipped into the skin of a refugee. Perhaps we should have done the same and got into training for the future: learn how to become invisible, disappear into a crowd, hug the walls, avoid eye contact, speak only when spoken to, bury our pride and close our hearts to humiliation and insults, throw our switchblades in the gutter, learn to keep in the background, to be nobody: another shadow, a stray dog, a lowly earthworm, or even a cockroach. That's it, yes, learn to be a cockroach.

8

A SORROW SHARED is a sorrow halved; Sister Benedicte's words came back to me as I cast my eyes around the sum of human distress gathered in such a tight circle. The cold had brought us closer without our noticing and we were now all huddled together. Pafadnam stank of musk like a marabout. We were paralyzed with cold, we could hardly feel our legs anymore from squatting or lying curled up behind that freezing, mossy rock for so long. What were we waiting for? No one knew. No one dared ask the trafficker. Did he even know? We had our doubts. We'd been stuck here like rats for hours, barely breathing for fear of being captured by the coastguard. It was an age since the scavengers had gone, leaving here and there their little piles of kelp.

"When are we going?" Reda complained with a noisy sigh.

My cousin was a champion at putting his foot in it. But this time I didn't really mind—it wasn't that bad to ask. We were exhausted, frozen stiff, eaten up with dread and uncertainty. Since the trafficker didn't react, Kacem Judi took it upon himself to respond.

"We will leave when the time comes, my boy."

"Will that be tonight or some other night?"

"Only the Boss can say."

"Well, why is he taking so long to make up his mind?"

"He has his reasons, my boy."

"He wouldn't want to share them with us, would he?"

Nuara's hand appeared and discreetly groped its way along the port side: she must have been short of air under there. That put an end to the pointless conversation between Reda and the talkative Algerian. Did he talk too much? I wondered. Kacem Judi did say a lot, but in fact he hardly ever talked about himself or his family. The only thing we knew about him for sure was that he'd fled Blida after a massacre that had wiped out about a hundred people, a lot of them women and children. Had he lost children of his own in the slaughter? Probably. One day in the café he'd started to eye a sweet-faced boy who was selling single cigarettes. He'd beckoned him over and handed him a ten-dirham note, without then helping himself to any of the cigarettes. He'd just stroked the boy's curly hair that fell over his hazel eyes and let him go. Watching this, I'd thought to myself that old Kacem had designs on the child; it's a classic, almost failsafe routine in these parts for men after young flesh: quickly growing used to the money, the boys keep coming back for more, and one evening they agree to go to see the tree where toffees grow, the lake of golden coins, and all the other marvels . . .

But once again I'd misjudged Kacem Judi, he didn't have anything perverse like that in mind. Just after the kid had left, I saw him awkwardly try to hide a few tears that had suddenly welled in his eyes. So then I guessed that the young cigarette-seller must have reminded him of a son, whose throat had been slit by a bearded fanatic one night in Blida. Well, that's what it looked like to me, because he couldn't just have been moved by the boy's fate, little brats like him were ten a penny round here: shoe-shine boys, kids with newspapers for hire or palming off smuggled goods, pilferers, glue-sniffers, not to mention whole cohorts of beggars, each more crippled than the last. No, there had to be some tragic story behind it. Perhaps he'd lost his entire family to the sacred khanjars of the men of God? Perhaps he'd found himself alone in an empty, devastated house? A house that had buried all the life in it, all the children's laughter, in its stone belly. How could a human being survive that? To be a husband, a father, an uncle, a friend, and then an hour later—the time it takes for a stroll in the moonlight—to be nothing. Nobody. A mass of grief. A knot of bitterness and remorse. Alone. Helpless. Hating yourself for living. Too weak to bury your family, or take your own life. Walking round in circles, banging your head against words, walls. Gouging your cheeks and tearing your face. Going to the sea and weeping. Roaming the damp sand, howling, and spitting in heaven's face. Running, walking, crawling for days and nights. Collapsing, sinking like wreckage into soothing, fitful exhaustion, waking up sobbing because a child's hazel eyes have ripped sleep's shadows, only to replace them with a dream that fades as suddenly as it came. Startled awake. Dragging your bones around again, and the sun on the sea looking like a blood-stain on God's hand. Meet a fisherman, tell yourself he's happy. Take his fresh water and grilled fish. Then go on walking, forever, with no purpose.

But I'm making things up; it's a habit of mine. Sister Benedicte used to say I had an unbridled imagination, that one day I'd be a writer. To write what, sister? Describe what? Poverty? People don't want to hear about that, let alone pay to have it shoved in their faces. Sister Benedicte would say that I could write about love then, the love of one's neighbor, the love of God. That same God, I suppose, in whose name Kacem Judi's children had had their throats slit?

Sister Benedicte is the person I love most in the world. I loved her from the moment I arrived at the School on the Hill, the embroidery school she ran with Sister Odette. I remember it as if it were yesterday. I was still a teenager and it was the first time I'd been to Marrakesh. Unlike my seven brothers and sisters, I was the only one given the chance to study. Being the eldest, my father experimented with sending me to the nearest school, five kilometers from the village. After me, he never tried again, but I'm not boasting when I say that right from the beginning I was an excellent pupil, despite the circumstances. My secret lay in paying attention to the teachers; I was a proper sponge, absorbing their very sighs. I didn't hang around to chat with my friends and, being good with my fists, I'd always be waiting outside if anyone dared disrupt the lessons.

My desire to learn was boundless. I had realized quite early on that school was the only way to get myself away from the village, from laboring in other people's fields, tending the sheep in the blazing heat, my father's fits of violence, the endless boredom every day, the tiny room where we all slept on top of each other. On winter mornings, when the sun was slow to rise, sometimes my courage would fail me at the thought of the long journey from our house to the college (that was the name we gave the three prefabricated classrooms, the headmaster, the Arabic teacher, and the two unhappy assistants stranded out there in the middle of nowhere). It was cold and I was very afraid of the dark. I would see monsters everywhere, lying in wait in the branches of the olive or eucalyptus trees. But still, I never missed a class. When my mother took pity on me—it happened two or three times a year—she'd let me borrow the she-ass as long as Reda came with me to bring it back. She was so afraid someone would steal her balding, scabby old donkey!

Sometimes, I'd go and wake Grandpa. He lived very near us, in a tiny adobe hut, with a hatch through which he sold candles, string, tea, sugar, biscuits, cigarettes, Coca-Cola, and chewing gum. I'd tap on the little window, which would open straight away. The old face would appear, split in two by his legendary toothless smile.

"Hello, little man," came the rasping voice. "Come on round the back!"

When I'd go in, he'd put in his dentures, light a candle, and give me a packet of biscuits that I'd make short work of. Then he'd drink his coffee, say his prayers, put on his coarse red woollen djellaba, and turning to me, say, "Are you sure you haven't left anything behind?"

I would shake my head, he'd take me by the hand, and, standing to attention, noisily clear his throat.

"Off we go, General!"

And we'd set off gaily on our journey, braving the ghosts all along the dark paths lined with brambles, well before the birds awoke.

He was funny, Grandpa. In the old days he'd worked as a doorman in the palace of a great governor who'd died soon after the departure of the French. Then the good working folk had pillaged the sumptuous residence and outbuildings and left them in ruins; Grandpa had only just escaped the lynch mob. After that he'd turned to business and lost everything he had, a lifetime's savings vanished into thin air in a matter of months. So he'd returned to the village, seen his three daughters married, buried his wife, and built a shop in which, in a way, he'd buried himself alive. Reda, his twin brother, and I would often hang around outside and he'd always throw us some sweets eventually; I'd be the first to grab them, though I always shared them with the other two, of course.

At fifteen, I got my secondary school certificate at the first go. Three of us passed. Mr. Romanchef, a Romanian who taught us mathematics, had solemnly announced the results, giving a short speech on the merits of each successful pupil. Sitting in the front row, I'd listened to him, staring intently at my inkwell. He'd hardly finished before hot tears flooded my throat, scalding my nose and eyes and spilling down my face. Hard as I tried to hold them back, I couldn't do it. I was angry with myself, me the tough guy, for showing such weakness. But what could I do, it was more than I could stand.

Mr. Romanchef, thinking they were tears of joy, had ignored me at first. Then, seeing that I didn't dry up, he came over to my bench and stroked my hair. A surprising thing for him to do, out of character. He crouched down and said softly, "What's up, my man?" His blue eyes, distorted by his thick-lensed glasses, were right by my face. His chestnut hair was almost touching me. He smelled of alcohol. Not the vinegary, stinking stuff they drink in the cantina on the main road, more like some expensive aniseed liqueur. After a while I managed to form an intelligible sentence that wasn't choked with sobs. I explained my situation—my father the peasant couldn't conceive of sending me to the city to continue my studies. I was refusing to sit the entrance exam for the police force. I hated the police, they terrified me. But this was my father's dream—and an order. I don't know where he'd got this diabolical idea, but it was all he thought about. He never missed an opportunity to glorify the forces of law and order, and already he imagined me, puffed up with my own importance, buttoned into a stone-colored uniform, treading the steep path to the village in my shiny, echoing boots, my mere presence making the locals tremble. I knew the sacrifices my father had made were as nothing beside the joy he would feel one morning when, seeing me in the main square, he'd say to some strangers, "See that man in uniform over there? Well, that's my son."

Mr. Romanchef kept me back after class for a little chat. I could tell by the tone of his voice that my status had changed from clever young peasant boy to the deeply gratifying one of adult, possessor of a certificate of secondary education. Mr. Romanchef was so proud; it hadn't been easy for him either, back home in Romania. He'd had to fight hard to go to university and leave his oppressed country. He promised to help me. The good Lord, he said, always gives opportunities to those who wish for them and who cling to their dreams, however inaccessible or irrational they may be. Because the truth is, dreams fade at low altitudes. They need space, blue sky, infinity. So if you hang on to them, you'll end up being carried along in their wake, up high, into skies of freedom. Of course life's hardships are the enemies of dreams, they never stop trying to capture them, weigh them down, clip their wings. But a dream you keep prisoner in your head for too long will fade and die as well. What could be more depressing than a dream dragging itself off to the cemetery of helplessness? Admittedly, dreams don't belong to anyone, they don't need anyone. But they'll go a little way with whoever courts them, and is persistent. Don't ever kill them . . .

As he spoke, Mr. Romanchef lifted his arms to the sky.
He stared at me, but I'm sure he didn't see me, he was looking right through me. Then he smiled as if to apologize
for his momentary absence and put his hand on mine. He
did have a friend, in Marrakesh, who might be able to help
me. (He preferred to speak to her first, as he didn't want
to run ahead of himself or give me false hopes; but it was a
charitable institution and he was reasonably confident.) So
I should go back and celebrate my success with my family;
it wasn't just anybody who could walk in with a certificate
in their back pocket!

I remember that when I came out of school that Friday
in June, I felt an irresistible urge to run. I tore off as fast
as my legs would carry me, without stopping or looking
around, in the opposite direction to the house. Even when
I was out of breath I kept on running, as if to avoid thinking. I only went back to the village late that evening. The
path was deserted, the night was dark. In the sky, a sliver of
moon smiled at the relentless song of the crickets and toads.
Seeing the light on in the shop, I went up, then hesitated. I
didn't want to disturb Grandpa or be a nuisance with my
moods. The radio was cheerfully blasting out waves of
laughter and applause. Hearing an animal coming toward
me, I hid in the shadows like a thief. I saw a man who seemed
to have travelled a long way; he looked exhausted, drowsing
on his donkey, which must have known the way by heart.
Suddenly the door opened and Grandpa appeared, armed
with a stick that he hid the moment he recognized me, in

case I'd be scared. He hadn't lost his doorman's instincts. My pale face worried him but, as usual, he didn't ask any questions. I didn't feel much like talking either. Going in, he lit a new candle, which he carefully stuck on the wax stub of the old one, served up Coca-Cola and madeleines and sat down on a stool to watch with some pleasure while I devoured the cakes. I bolted them down, because I hadn't eaten all day. Then he laid out a blanket next to his and put his thick, heavy djellaba over me, and I curled up like a cat in its warmth. Grandpa stroked my hair a long while, murmuring prayers and fingering his amber prayer beads.

At school on Monday, I saw Mr. Romanchef coming towards me in the distance, beaming all over his ruddy face. He was nodding yes with his head and I trembled at the thought that this yes wasn't meant for me, but for someone else I hadn't noticed. My heart pounding, I turned round every which way and once I was sure, threw myself into my teacher's arms. He hugged me tightly. "You see, the Lord is good to those who try!" A wave of happiness swept over me, a peculiar feeling I'd never had before—it felt the way it would right now, in the depths of this gloomy night, looking at this clammy rock and the trafficker's black, motionless shadow, if someone were to ride up on a white horse and give me a passport with a different visa on every page—the whole world at my fingertips. An open, welcoming world. For me, just for me.

Door to door, it was about a hundred kilometers from the village to the establishment known as the School on the

Hill, yet between walking, bus, and taxi, it took Grandpa and me the whole day. It was swelteringly hot and the air was made heavier by one of those storms that hug the ground and never break. The bus stank of Bedouin. But Grandpa, although he was wearing his woollen djellaba, hardly seemed to feel the heat. My chest tight with a thousand vague misgivings, I tried to shake off the swarm of dark thoughts that troubled me. The seats were so close together I got pins and needles in my legs; I felt exhausted the whole way. It wasn't until the first palm trees came into sight that I revived: they were slender and gracious on their stemlike trunks, proudly raising their fronds to the sky.

Perched on one foot between two of the ramparts' crenellations, a motionless stork watched us go by. The setting sun softened the glare of colors, blurring hard contours, slowing time, veiling everything in a sweet air of mystery. At last the city! The miracle of the city, jealously protected by its walls! Its huge avenues lined with bitter orange trees, its monumental fountains gushing up from the asphalt, ringed with asphodels and marigolds, its hundreds of cafés huddled together, packed with effete, indolent customers, its cinemas, its fairy-tale shop windows, its signs and lights. Then the medina, the dense, animated crowds in a fever of noise and calls, enveloped in the aromas of grilled meat, mint, and spices that were overpowering, as if everyone was carrying a meal in the hood of his djellaba.

Grandpa, who was escorting me to my new home, had lived here for thirty years, so the labyrinth of alleyways in the medina was no mystery to him. We plunged into that whirl of people, animals, bicycles, motorbikes, handcarts, carriages with kids hanging from the back, the drivers beating them off, cracking their fearsome whips on the sides. With his pouch tucked under his arm, Grandpa didn't let go of my hand until we'd reached the School on the Hill. He'd warned me beforehand that he had no desire to meet the sisters. What would he have to say to them? In any case, he didn't speak their language. So we'd barely arrived before he hurried off, hid behind a leafy tree, and signalled to me to ring the bell. Which I didn't do immediately but stood there, gazing at the impressive garden gate. It was a real curiosity, a bank of lances welded together, their sharp blades pointing at the sky. It looked like a row of sentries lined up behind a massive shield that would have made any thief lose heart. The shards of glass and barbed wire we used at home seemed suddenly ridiculous and old-fashioned. I pulled on the bell, timidly at first, then more firmly. Sister Odette came out first, closely followed by Sister Benedicte. Both were dressed in white, a dazzling white that matched their pure, clear faces, which exuded the serenity and kindness of the wise. Sister Odette smiled as she drew back the heavy, threatening gate.

"So it's you, Aziz," she said, kissing me on both cheeks.

"Yes, ma'am."

"Mr. Romanchef has told us so many good things about you."

I looked down as the blood rushed to my face.

"Welcome to your new home," added Sister Benedicte after kissing me on both cheeks as well.

I wasn't used to women cosseting me; it wasn't unpleasant. The sisters asked me to follow them. I turned round to wave to Grandpa, but he'd gone. He'd scuttled off, as if ashamed of our poverty. He who never tired of telling us that the upper hand, the one that gives, is a thousand times superior to the lower, the one that receives; he, the former doorman to a governor, had been reduced to placing his grandson in a charitable institution.

With a lump in my throat, I entered the School on the Hill, and they showed me my room, at the far end of the courtyard, between Ali's room—a gardener who was a war veteran—and the garage. It was a dream room, more comfortable than I could ever have hoped: a proper bed, a teacher's desk, an electric lamp, mauve velvet curtains, a wardrobe made of precious wood, and lastly a door that led to a shower room tiled all the way up to the ceiling. Cold water. Hot water. What bliss!

I didn't want to put my filthy bag on the clean mosaic floor, so I slipped it into the plastic bag the sisters had handed me. They'd suggested I put all my clothes in as well, including the ones I had on; something to do with lice, probably. Until I got them back I could wear the blue and grey striped cotton pajamas that were folded under the pillow. I put them on straight after the shower, which I made last for an eternity. The hot water never, ever ran out!

When I sat down on my bed I had the fright of my life, a crazy, indescribable feeling of falling. I felt I was being swallowed up by the bedding, trapped by my own struggling. Trembling, I clutched at the edge of the bed to stop myself sinking. But the more I fought, the farther I fell, as though I was being sucked under by an octopus. I bit the sheet so as not to cry out. Here I was, having only known hard straw mats and carpets woven by my mother, tricked by the treacherous springs of a wire bed! It didn't last long, but long enough, at any rate, for me to decide to sleep on the floor, that first night at the School on the Hill.

9

THE BOSS EASED back the hood of his oilskin and listened. We did the same. A faint, broken sound of barking dogs came from far away, carried on a hot, dry wind like the chergui. It might have stayed just one of those vague echoes, background noise, if the trafficker's shadow hadn't suddenly changed shape. He imposed silence with a movement of his big sailor's hands and stood up. Wetting his finger, he tried to work out where the sound was coming from, but the wind was no help, it was blowing in all directions.

Wrapped in my burnous, eyes open and teeth no longer chattering, Reda had laid his head on my shoulder. He seemed to have admitted defeat and given up, not even trying to struggle against this dense night that stretched on endlessly, blotting out his future. The invisible thread that bound him to the Great Dream had snapped; he was already breathing the thin but untroubled air of those without ambition. Reda felt powerless; we all did.

Defying the trafficker's orders, Yarcé began to hum a weird lament, as though to ward off bad luck. Pafadnam joined in. Although barely audible, it was very beautiful, a noble, plaintive melody rising from somewhere deep inside them. Not having a bamboula drum, Yarcé tapped on his knees, and if he'd dared, Pafadnam would definitely have stood up and danced around us. I think I would too, if only to warm myself up a little. The trafficker didn't object because Yarcé, despite his reserve and the way he kept to himself, had still earned all our respect. There are people like him whose silence is imbued with intelligence and an imperceptible resolve, who have no need to twist themselves out of shape to give weight to their presence.

He was young, Yarcé, and not very tall, but there was something in his eyes that instantly set him above us. He had an oval face, regular features and very short hair, shaved at the sides, and, unlike his countryman, he'd arrived in Tangier three years earlier. He'd got a job as a masseur for an English multimillionaire who owned several hunting lodges in Africa and a sumptuous house in the middle of the medina, a riad that had once belonged to a powerful pasha, now completely renovated and decorated in the old style by a famous architect. There, Yarcé had had to knead and pummel the fat, milky flesh of an endless succession of moaning, ugly, white grandees who smelled like corpses. Anyway, as far as Yarcé was concerned, whites in general had the bland, sickly odor of cadavers. One day he showed us the mansion in a faded old copy of an architectural review that he carried around with him like a curriculum vitae. It had a photo of him; he was standing up very straight with his chest thrust out, in front of a square door carved in different colored woods, smartly done up like a doorman in dark red velvet pantaloons and waistcoat, white shirt with billowing sleeves, fez, and chamois slippers. In another photo there was a shot of him from the back in the middle of a flower-filled patio near an intricately ornamented marble fountain, ostentatiously proffering a pewter teapot to serve invisible guests. He'd been chosen specially because he was the only black man in the house, to give a hint of the exotic; his dark, servile silhouette added nostalgia, evoking a vanished colonial past. The malicious gossips of the Café France had it that Yarcé and the Englishman had been lovers, not that the Malian gave any sign of such an inclination, but who knows, with masseurs or hairdressers you never can tell. One thing was certain, the Englishman had contracted a horrible disease from his hunting in Africa, and then Yarcé had found himself out on the street, for there was no one to massage anymore, and the swarm of heirs that had fallen on the house soon showed him the door. This was how he'd ended up in the flophouse where a happy chance had led him to Morad.

Yarcé had a tidy sum put by; three long years of patient saving, penny by penny, had earned him the European Deportee's instant and heartfelt friendship. Before his death, the Englishman had promised to take him to

London and Paris one day, but there you go, he'd departed this life too soon and didn't give much warning. Whereas Morad, like a lifeline, was very much present and full of tempting plans for his Malian brother. Crossing the Strait? A mere formality! A piddling five thousand French francs and buenos días España! After that, one night in a comfy couchette on the express train and you wake up in Hendaye, refreshed and full of energy, to radiant sunshine. Pepe, the Spanish partner he'd give the second half of the payment to, would take care of the rest: a lovely little ramble over the Pyrenees, bypassing border controls, and hey presto! Yes sirree, it was child's play. He, Yarcé Bukari, wouldn't be the first nor the last to take advantage of this route, the system was tried and tested, it was as good as infallible. Morad had used it three times himself as a would-be immigrant, and then, as he grew older, he'd switched over, the way a footballer turns coach. He liked to cultivate this metaphor, which he must have thought most poetic. "An *international* player!" he'd add. This witticism always broke the ice.

In the Café France, Morad's tales of his erstwhile adventures were inexhaustible. He had our jaws dropping at stories that were both bizarre and thrilling. I liked the one about the brothel he'd visit on the weekends on his day off. In Barbès, on the top floor of a derelict building, someone had opened a blow-up doll service exclusively for African immigrants. It was twenty francs a go, with a glass of mint tea thrown in. Ten times cheaper than Saint-Denis with, moreover, the invaluable advantage of convenience—selling points that in no time had garnered a faithful, mostly North African clientele. Sometimes you'd see black men queuing on the narrow staircase too, but there were never that many. The young ladies waited for them, fresh-faced, alluring and submissive, permitting kisses, caresses, and the most acrobatic of bedroom romps. They had delightful names discreetly inscribed on their temples, in case it took some men's fancy to spice up their lovemaking with a little endearment or confidence. Morad had a thing for Lilli, a superb blonde with enormous, firm breasts who stuck out a fleshy little tongue, the color of strawberries. On the days he was racked with homesickness—a nostalgia that never lasted long—he'd have Aisha, a brunette with eyes like coals, lowered lashes, and a shy smile fixed for eternity on her full lips. On a good night, he'd pay for the two of them, one after the other. When Mr. Larbi, the Tunisian manager, would agree to a wholesale price, he'd have Tsu as well, a Chinese girl with a slanted, tight sex. In the secrecy of my own heart, I thought that once I'd reached France, I was definitely going to take a walk around Barbès, where there were so many curious things to discover . . .

The trafficker again ordered us to keep quiet. The streaks of sweat gleaming under his hood made us take the dog's barking seriously; it was getting closer.

"It's a German shepherd," said Pafadnam in a hoarse whisper. "Just one. That means two or three coastguards, maybe. We'll have to hide."

"What about the mother?" asked Kacem Judi.

"We leave her," said Pafadnam.

"What do you mean, leave her?" the Algerian exclaimed. "There's a baby under there."

"Exactly. If he starts bawling, we're all screwed."

"They're asleep," mediated Yarcé. "Pafadnam's right, we shouldn't wake them. Anyway, the child has nothing to fear, the angels are watching over him."

Kacem Judi nodded, resignedly. He didn't want us to leave Nuara under the boat. As for the angels, he knew only too well that they'd stopped watching over anyone long ago.

We got up quickly and followed the trafficker to a sand dune covered in tall sharp grass, a couple of hundred meters from the boat, which at that distance merged with the rocks. The Boss lay down on his stomach; we copied him. It was better there, the wind hardly blew between the dunes and the sand was dry—cold but dry. I wondered why we hadn't hidden there in the first place.

Reda's composure surprised me; in my late father's burnous, which suited him wonderfully, he looked like a sheikh meditating in the middle of the desert. Yussef had left his bag by the boat, but there was no question of going back for it now. The barking was very close. Kacem Judi was still upset. He seemed really worried about Nuara and the baby. I wasn't that calm either; my cousin's peaceful appearance bothered me. "Still waters run deep," Sister Benedicte always said. Yarcé whispered something to the Boss, who merely tilted his hood in agreement. I strained to hear what he said, but had to give up.

Suddenly we saw the beast, a German shepherd the size of an ass's foal. The mist had thinned, leaving gaps through which a bright moon appeared, full and proud. As I stared at it, I thought I saw the outline of Grandpa's face. Was he trying to warn me of some sort of danger? The dog was prowling round the boat, sniffing here and there; then he started digging and snarling. Just in time, the trafficker stopped Kacem Judi from playing the hero; seizing his hand, he checked him without even looking up, as if the effort cost him nothing, then let go without a sound. For a moment Kacem Judi seemed paralyzed by the chill of the trafficker's hand. Intoning a verse from the Koran to drive off Satan, he sat back down in pained silence. Yarcé patted him on the back. "You'd have got us all killed" he murmured.

I kept on glancing over at Reda, who looked as if he'd smoked a bale of kif. He didn't seem in the least concerned by the situation, but then had he ever been concerned by anything?

Stung by some insect as he was digging furiously and growling, the German shepherd suddenly let out a hideous yelping, so loud that any coastguard in a three-kilometer radius would have heard it. From where we were it was difficult to make out what exactly was happening, but we could see the dog leaping and banging itself against the boat again and again. The harder its head hit the wood, the more it howled, shaking its body in a cloud of sand, whimpering like someone being tortured. I almost felt sorry for it, then I remembered it was after me too, so along with my companions I set my mind to hating it and wanting it dead.

The trafficker scanned the area, looking out for people. Nothing. There was no sign of life. The howling eventually died down and then stopped. Even the wind had dropped, as if to confer on the deadly silence all the solemnity it deserved. Stuck against the side of the boat, the dog had stopped moving. Still, we waited a good quarter of an hour before going back. Amazed, we found that the dangerous German shepherd was just a pathetic stray dog, so typical of Morocco, lying on the sand with its jaw smashed in. When we lifted up the hull, Nuara was still holding on to one of its paws; she must have bitten it right through to the bone, her mouth was smeared with blood. We had trouble making her let go, her hand was gripping the fur so tightly. How petrified she must have been to take on the dog like that. Kacem Judi knelt down beside her, took a handkerchief from his pocket and wiped her mouth. He put his hand over hers, murmuring, "It's over now, my dear, it's over."

The dog was probably still breathing when the trafficker buried it.

10

THE BLOOD AROUND Nuara's mouth reminded me of Morad's dream. Dream? Nightmare, more like.

The European Deportee had told us about it one evening, stoned out of his head after a long day's smoking. I think he'd even had a teaspoon or two of majoun, otherwise he probably wouldn't have said a thing. Because it didn't exactly serve his cause as a trafficker.

We were in the Café France, sitting as usual at the back table. Even though night was coming on, there were masses of flies, drawn by the over-sugared, syrupy tea; they were maneuvering dangerously in our glasses where they seemed to like it. We'd given up shooing them away, so we could concentrate properly on Morad, whose drawling voice, hoarse with smoke and emotion, made him sound like a character in a radio soap. His sleepy eyes lit up with a distant, feverish flame when he talked about Mr. José, the manager of Chez Albert.

A gourmet (and greedy with it), this big fat fellow had quite a likeable, chubby-cheeked face with a moustache tapering into a carefully groomed little goatee beard that framed a pair of thick, wet lips. When he ate, he wolfed down his food, his gaping mouth revealing a chasm of crimson flesh. His enormous appetite gave everyone the creeps. Mr. José liked to have his meals in the kitchen with the rest of the staff. It was his way of reminding everyone that although he'd risen to the position of manager by the sweat of his brow, that didn't mean he was going to disown his working-class roots. In fact he advertised them at every opportunity, to make it abundantly clear that anyone willing to put their back into it could end up like him.

Momo understood that. He himself had gone from bogus tourist guide in Marrakesh, dodging shady policemen who'd fined him whenever they could, to illegal dishwasher in the heart of the French capital, hunted by the courageous riot police, proud protectors of the nation. He'd certainly come a long way! From there to becoming owner of a restaurant, well, that might be pushing it a bit. No, he had no such ambition. At the very most if, by some miracle, he managed to obtain a residence permit—with savings he couldn't possibly make—he'd like to be a street vendor, selling crêpes and hot chestnuts in the winter, and ice cream and lemonade in summer, like the Greek guy in rue Monsieur-le-Prince who always had a queue. Momo sometimes stopped by for a Nutella crêpe. He adored them, but fifteen francs, that was daylight robbery!

So, anyway, back to the dream, or rather the nightmare. It came back night after night—same scene, same location, same images, same helplessness, same characters, same bloodlust, give or take a mouthful.

It began like this: Momo and Mr. José are driving along in a red convertible, out for a spin on a strangely deserted Champs-Élysées. The wind and the sound of the wheels on the Paris streets accompany them. Momo gazes at the blue sky. Not a trace of cloud, not one bird. Mr. José's scarf flies off. They park in front of an empty café, get out, and sit down on the terrace. A pallid waiter with bloodshot eyes places two glasses of bitter almond liqueur on the table. Mr. José talks and talks. Momo can't hear him, all he can see is his outsize, open mouth where, instead of teeth, there's an infinite number of forks. The glittering, grinding stainless steel thrashes out a cascade of muddled words whose vague echo Momo begins to catch, just about; the voice is metallic yet soft, harsh and bewitching, irresistible. Momo lets himself be swept along, opens his heart, swallows the words, absorbs their sense, and, inevitably, agrees with them. He clinks glasses with the boss and swigs the almond liqueur, which sets his throat on fire.

The waiter serves them again and they go on drinking. Mr. José's eyes are red like the waiter's, saliva dribbles from his mouth. He's had the chance to try everything up till now, in his life, everything but human flesh. And the thing is, he craves it, this flesh, he craves it deeply, avidly, desperately, he's been dreaming about it for years. If Momo would give up even just one of his toes—with so many, what does it matter?—Mr. José would be eternally grateful to him. He is prepared to make any sacrifice to appease this raging desire that's tormented him for so long. One yes, just one little whispered yes, and Momo would find himself the beneficiary of endless favors and incalculable privileges: he could work in the dining room, for instance (Benoit's job will soon be free, he's not right for it anymore, quite a few customers have complained about his rude manner, his total lack of charm), or he could have a new place to live. Mr. José owns a fine two-room apartment on the third floor that could be his. Or perhaps a substantial raise in salary, or even—but in that case he'd have to part with at least a thigh—a residence permit. There's that police inspector, Mr. Paul, who often eats in the restaurant and always has as many aperitifs and liqueurs as he wants, on the house. Mr. José could have a word with him. Nothing's impossible when you show you are willing, when you're generous. Anyway, a finger, what's that? A little bit of nothing, a pathetic scrap of flesh and bone that sooner or later will end up food for the worms, a complete waste. The truth is— the sad, the old, the only truth—we all inescapably return to the earth. Were Mr. José to eat one of Momo's fingers, it would only be a matter of time before dust returned to dust. Might as well make good use of it while you're alive, make the most of yourself right up till the last moment . . .

To his great surprise, Momo found he could easily survive the loss of a toe from each foot. It barely affected his sense of balance, as he'd originally feared. In return, he was assigned the position he so coveted, replacing Benoit, his secret rival. Lord how Momo shone, decked out as maître d', in his black waistcoat and trousers, his white shirt and bow tie, proudly making his entrance into the dining room, showing off the lavish tools of the trade laid on by the boss: a corkscrew on a thin chain like a fob watch's, a gold-plated Dupont lighter, a gold Montblanc fountain pen, a spiral vellum notebook, and a carefully ironed napkin over his left arm. He flitted from table to table, taking an order here, serving dishes there, bending over backward to ensure no one was kept waiting. In the beginning, it was tremendously exciting; he felt noticed, admired, adored by the customers, with whom he never failed to share a little joke. It was all "If you please, Mr. Momo," and "Thank you, Mr. Momo." For fun, for the thrill of it, he'd even go over and chat with Inspector Paul. Oh he wasn't at all the tough, harsh character Momo used to glimpse through the serving hatch in the days when he'd been a mere dishwasher; Mr. Paul was a charming creature, quite easygoing for a policeman. Of course he was on familiar terms with Momo, like all the regulars, and he would say, "Thank you, young man!" in his warm, gravelly voice, each time he was served his brandy. He drank like a fish, Mr. Paul, without ever appearing in the least bit drunk. His features simply softened; a veil of tenderness, light as silk, blurred their natural severity, as if he were ready to love the entire planet, thieves and murderers included.

At the bar, sitting behind the till, Mr. José devoured Momo with his greedy bloodshot eyes, scrutinizing the young maître d's frail body as he patrolled the vast, teeming room. In order to earn the two-bedroom apartment on the third floor, Momo had had to concede another part of his body. It hadn't been an easy choice; after much negotiation with Mr. José, they'd agreed on the rest of the toes, plus two reasonably thick slices out of his buttocks, not too much to spoil his figure. Again, the inconvenience was pretty minor: his walk had altered slightly and he had to sit down at a slant, but nothing really nasty. And besides, his new lodgings were magnificent. The bedroom was padded like a cocoon, with fabric on the walls and a thick wool carpet and a double bed so soft and cozy it caressed every part of his body. The living room was like the ones in magazines, it had a black leather sofa, an armchair, a fireplace, coffee tables, a library, pictures, a standard lamp, a polished wooden floor, moldings on the ceiling. And last of all a window, a large, superb window that looked out on rue Mazarine. Momo would sit there for hours on end watching people go by, ogling the gorgeous creatures fresh from some northern paradise.

Oh, those peaceful days when, relieved of the knot of anguish wedged in the hollow of his chest, he could forget the cops and their shiftiness, other people and their pettiness, the hordes of skinheads who'd go out Arab-bashing all night, every night. Momo forgot about it all. He had a pair of binoculars—another gift from the boss—with which he'd practically moved into the building opposite. Using them was a real joy; every little window had its own story, its intrigues, its joys and sorrows, its outbursts, its arguments and reconciliations, its calm and fury, its whole life. Momo couldn't hear what was said behind the window panes or tulle curtains, but he could guess at everything. Even if it weren't true, he pretended to believe it.

Having acquired a taste for Momo's flesh, Mr. José would ask for more each day and, grown used to luxury, Momo would comply. Curiously, the fact of being eaten wasn't as horrible as he might have imagined. It even gave him an erotic thrill he didn't dare admit to himself; it was almost orgasmic. So he'd traded one arm for a major pay rise, the other for the promise of a residence permit, then both legs when it arrived. In this way he'd gradually used up almost the whole of his body; all he had left was his head with its frizzy hair, his dark eyes and his mouth, which, despite everything, went on smiling.

The only work his condition now permitted him was on reception. On a feather pillow covered in dark red velvet, his head was placed on the counter by the till near the door, a strategic position enabling him to oversee almost the entire room. He'd welcome the customers as they came in, starving and often without a reservation, thank those who, tipsy and with full bellies, were slowly setting off home again, and he'd give directions to the cloakroom and toilets to whoever needed them. In between, he'd chat to the barman, all the while glancing furtively over at Mr.

José, who was always busy doing and redoing his accounts. In the evening he was put in a straw basket and carried up to his apartment. Garcia usually took on this job, and would climb the three floors puffing and blowing like an old steam engine, stopping every ten steps for a little rest. Momo liked to be put on his pillow near the window, in the half-light of the luminous signs, which blinked all night long, for him and all the ghosts.

His dream, no, his nightmare would stop there—well, almost always. The night before his arrest, it had gone differently. Had he accelerated his downfall with his desperate desire to know the end of the dream? Had he inadvertently encouraged the nightmare to come true by upsetting the sly game of whichever little devils were enjoying tormenting him? Had he violated a code, transgressed some mysterious law? Today, when he thinks back, he still tells himself he should never have gone back to sleep that night. He'd have done better to get up as he usually did, wipe his face all running with sweat, smoke a cigarette, smile at the goddesses on the walls of his studio apartment, and thank the Lord for letting him still be in one piece—a dishwasher, a peeler of vegetables, illegal, displaced, anything you like, but whole! But no, he had sunk back into sleep. Worse, he had tried so hard to assimilate this strange story that he'd managed to storm the dream's gates, blundering in with his heavy boots.

So he'd rejoined his head, up there on the pillow by the window. The street was quiet, the neon signs competing over which could project its message furthest. A few black guys were trotting behind a garbage truck driven by a white man; they were attaching the bottle-green trash cans that a mechanical arm then lifted and tipped into the truck, which instantly chewed up and swallowed their contents like a monstrous mouth. Momo told himself that they obviously hadn't found anyone to snack on them, otherwise they'd be comfortably settled in the warmth on a pillow like him, watching other black men running after a municipal garbage truck.

Mr. José appeared, his paunch leading the way, which none of his ample jackets could contain any more. He was saying something, but the voices of the excited garbagemen at the foot of the building drowned him out. He leaned over Momo and murmured in his ear, "I don't like heads. Calves' heads. Pigs' heads. None of them."

"Nor do I," replied Momo.

"Yours disgusts me."

"It disgusts me too."

"You're no use here anymore."

"I know."

"What am I going to do with you, I wonder?"

"Eat me, Mr. José. For the love of God, eat me. I'm so tired!"

Opening the window, the boss surprised a garbageman pissing down below, by the restaurant door. He flew into a rage, spitting, "Dirty nigger!", "Dirty Arab!", dirty anything foreign that came into his head. Seizing Momo's head by the hair, he flung it out with all his strength. It was a long fall, it seemed it would never end, as if the frizzy-haired little head was falling from the seventh heaven. Momo shut his eyes to stop the dizziness. The wind lashed his face as he struggled to get out of the nightmare before hitting the ground. But the gate he'd stormed a few hours earlier was resisting him now. No way he could wrench it open again. A prisoner in his own dream, he kept on falling, pursued by the boss's yells, which, mingled with the garbagemen's racket, became unbearable: shrieks, furious insults, an evil hyena laughing. Had he still had a heart, it would have been pumping hard. Momo awoke just as the truck's monstrous jaws were pulverizing his broken skull with a dull crunch.

This dream, no, this nightmare, did not bode well; it wouldn't be long before he, Momo, Chez Albert's little fuzzhead, found that out.

11

"'IT'S THE QUIET ones you have to watch," Sister Benedicte would maintain. "They're people who spend too long cut off inside themselves. You have to read their expressions carefully, the way they move their lips and hands. It's simple, really," she'd explain. "The eyes, the lips and the hands have their own autonomy, so they respond more to raw feelings and emotion than to the upbringing and affectations of the person supposedly in charge of them."

But when someone's as taciturn as the trafficker and, what's more, utterly motionless under an enormous green oilskin, there's no way to fathom his silence. Not that we hadn't all had a go. But, apart from Yarcé, no one had managed to establish contact with him for more than thirty seconds without being interrupted by growls or a raised fist. Kacem Judi could vouch for that; so could Reda.

After the burial of the dog, Nuara had not gone back under the boat. Since then she'd breathed fresh air just the same as the rest of us and tried not to worry about her baby crying; anyway, he was fast asleep, his fists clenched. The heroism she'd shown defending herself against the dog had earned her everyone's admiration and respect; a woman who can draw blood biting a mutt's leg is perfectly capable of ripping your balls off.

The trafficker stood up and went down to the sea's edge. For a moment he peered into the shadows, as if he could see something of interest. When he returned, a thinly disguised air of satisfaction gave a little spring to his step.

"We leave in one hour," he said, with no further comment.

He cleared his throat noisily and spat a big greenish globule onto the sand.

We looked at each other, joyful but afraid.

"What have we done to deserve this great news?" Reda ventured.

I slipped my hand under the burnous and pinched my cousin hard; he let out a yelp and then was silent. That's how he was, Reda, like one of those poodles that never stop yapping, and the more scared he got, the less he could contain himself. He was always landing us in it. The trafficker acted as if he hadn't heard. He came up, pushed the boat back over and sat down between Pafadnam and Yarcé, pulling down the hood of his oilskin.

Kacem Judi explained that the Boss must have been given the signal from the Spanish trawler that we were going to board halfway across. Things were looking pretty good, he added. It wasn't yet midnight. Between the boat and the trawler, the crossing would take around four hours. We were on schedule; the main thing was to be in Algeciras before daybreak.

That had to be a fine sight, Algeciras at dawn, coming into shore under a cloudless sky. I saw myself as a conquering hero at the prow, chest thrown out, ready to take on all the demons of the West. Once we were on dry land, I'd go and set the sultry hearts of the Andalusian women on fire. Morad had made them seem the most seductive, the most delicious, the most bewitching women on earth. Houris, more graceful than the Berber women of Khenifra, more charming than the Azrou women, and more coquettish than the beauties of Fez. Looking up from their ample bosoms, their eyelids fluttering after a wild flamenco, one glance could bring any man to his knees, he claimed. Well, I was ready to surrender right now, give myself up bound hand and foot and grovel at their feet for as long as it took.

One hour left before throwing ourselves blindly into the great adventure, quietly slipping into a new life, donning its clothes, embracing its hours and days, so we could be born again somewhere else, change our skin, our air, our world, start everything again from scratch. One more hour and we could shrug off our mud-caked memories, drive the adobe hovels out of our minds, forget the barren fields, the life of struggle, poverty and distress. One hour, Lord, just one little hour, and, eyes closed, we'd be carried away on the tides of this forbidden dream.

In the tumult of my mind I sometimes heard Sister Benedicte's voice, as if the angel she had no doubt become was silently entering my head, taking up residence amongst my chaotic thoughts and whispering soothing, reasonable, wise words to me.

If she were still alive, I don't think I ever would have left the School on the Hill; the three years I'd spent there had been by far the happiest of my life. I had practically no contact with the outside world. Saint Benedicte—as Father Ali and I used to call her as a joke—had enrolled me in the Victor Hugo Lycée, through people she knew, first just to sit in, and then, when I began to do well, as a student in my own right. Sister Benedicte had made it her duty to make up for how much I'd fallen behind over the years at my prefabricated school. She'd begun by having me cram the entire Pink Library, then the Green one, and so on until I'd exhausted all the colors of the rainbow. As my reading improved, she gave me more interesting books, books that were right for my age, that spoke to me and gave me a real taste for reading. I often had the feeling that a particular author knew me personally, that he could see me as I see you, by the light of a candle, down the centuries, that his words encompassed my own sensations, that he gave them wings and, smiling at me from the fortress of his solitude, watched them fly off toward me.

The hardest part, of course, was always summarizing these books for Sister Benedicte at the end of every week. She'd summon me to her office on the second floor of the main building, above the classroom where fifty or so young girls used to sit, bent over their embroidery hoops. Like a cock in a henhouse, my presence never failed to disturb them. I'd cross the vast room followed by whispers, muffled laughter, and a wall of withering looks anticipating my clumsiness; if I didn't slip on the shiny tiled floor, I'd collide with a table, drop my book, or suddenly notice my fly was undone. Crossing that hall was a real calvary. Sister Odette was often forced to intervene with a clap of her hands: "Enough, young ladies, back to work!" And she'd smile at me as I went into the corridor to take the staircase at the far end.

Sister Benedicte's office was a restful place. It was a pretty room, equipped with a cherry-wood bookcase that covered a long stretch of wall and sagged under the weight of its expensively bound books. There were two soft leather armchairs that instantly sent you to sleep, on either side of a writing desk, or her bonheur-du-jour, as she coyly referred to it. A large window overlooked the garden; if you leaned slightly to the right you could see my room. Sister Benedicte would rest her head on the back of her rocking chair, facing the cross on which Christ suffered for eternity, and, rocking back and forth, her eyes half-closed, she'd say, "I'm listening, my boy." Then I had to begin at the beginning.

I'm not just saying it, but Sister Benedicte really had read everything. It was impossible to trick her, her phenomenal memory retained even the tiniest details. When, out of laziness, I hadn't finished a book by Sunday afternoon and I'd invent a plausible ending so as not to upset her, she'd let me go on to the end and then say with gentle irony, "I think Mr. Dumas saw the dénouement rather differently," or "Goodness me! Saint-Exupéry would have liked that." Or even, when I'd made a real hash of it, she'd pretend to be indignant and murmur, "A little imagination, Aziz dear, good Mr. Maupassant must be turning in his grave!"

Outside of classes and homework, I'd go and lend a hand to Father Ali, who had the room next to mine and was my friend. Father Ali was a true master of the floral arts, judging by the splendid garden of the School on the Hill, which earned him praise from every quarter, especially from Sister Odette, whose love of God only just surpassed her love of flowers. Father Ali would often make up bouquets that I'd take to her myself in the embroidery room. She'd welcome me with her limpid smile, dropping everything to arrange them at once in a vase. Then she'd make me repeat the flowers' names, not the Latin terms but their popular ones: cockscomb, marvel of Peru, snapdragon, meadow-sweet, nymph's thigh lilies, love-lies-bleeding, bear's ear, guelder-rose, or larkspur—a whole string of funny names that might have been Sioux and were all easy to remember. I had a weakness for poppies, half-mourning roses, and— my favorite of all—the proud orchids.

A native of Mgouna, Ali had been born and had grown up among roses, until one morning when he was enlisted and taken off to Indochina to fight people he hadn't known existed until then. Later he wound up in Germany and after that, Algeria. For him, the faceless enemy was always camped up ahead, on the other side of a mountain or forest, in the ruins of a dead city. He'd list conflicts in which he claimed to have participated, but of which there was no trace in the history books.

One evening, as he recounted his expeditions around the world, I'd said, "Tell me, Father Ali, with all that travelling, you must know a lot about geography."

"Geography, you say? Yes, yes, hang on, it's coming back to me, we went there a long time ago. Unfortunately, our stay there was cut short by the fighting that broke out in Indochina . . ."

After that, I began to put Father Ali's remarks in perspective. Still, I enjoyed listening to him dreaming of his past, all those years over which he'd had no control whatsoever, tossed from one event to the next, from one uncertainty to another. As he recalled them, he made me think of a bystander lost in his own history.

One morning, trucks had rolled up in his village. He was just sixteen. He vaguely remembered a cloud of dust, galloping horses, and excited children shouting. The sheikh, the governor, and the Arab soldiers had been first to arrive. The governor's tents had been put up, one of them a lavish affair with carpets, hangings, cushions, low tables—the works. The crier had assembled the entire village. Some high-ranking French officers, to whom everyone kowtowed, had appeared like ghosts in a long black car; the governor had greeted them obsequiously before launching into an impassioned speech, explaining to the stupefied

crowd that imminent danger was threatening the mother-
land, that their dear protectors had need of them and their
legendary bravery: all men of honor should join with the
French forces without delay to overcome the invader. "The
country's fate is in your hands," he'd concluded. Then it
was the sheikh's turn to speak; backing up the first speak-
er's words, he went one better, announcing that his own
son would be first to sign up and that, had he the physical
strength, he himself wouldn't have hesitated for a second.

That was how young Ali had found himself, along with
many others, queuing in front of a medical tent where, in
a matter of minutes, they'd pronounced him in excellent
health, no problems with his teeth, and so in perfect condition to go off and die on a battlefield. He'd been given the
go-ahead to put his fingerprints on several forms, thereby
sealing his allegiance to the Spahi corps for an unspeci-
fied length of time. From being a simple Bedouin growing
his flowers in the sun, swathed in a shabby djellaba, Ali
found himself metamorphosed into a modern man, with a
brilliant red and blue uniform, a superb mount in shining
harness, and a rifle and bayonet that made all the boys in
the village green with envy.

Father Ali bore an uncanny resemblance to Grandpa,
especially when he took out his false teeth. Both their
voices had that comforting softness, that even, gentle tone
of people who never lose their temper. We used to eat our
meals together in the kitchen, where we were looked after
by Lalla Fatima, the very fat and funny mistress of the

kitchen, who gave in to most of our whims. She'd often come and sit at our table to watch us try her delicacies: lentils with dried meat, lambs' brains in garlic, or eggplant purée with chili. Thirty years in her job had invested her with absolute power at the School on the Hill. Whilst endlessly repeating that gluttony is a mortal sin, the sisters refused her nothing, even when she demanded spices that we'd have to track down from the most obscure corners of the casbah. Father Ali and I would set off on his old bike, with me sitting sidesaddle on the bar while he, perched on the saddle, would pedal like a strapping youngster, shouting, "Gangway! Gangway!" We'd criss-cross the city, threading through winding alleys packed with people, eyes peeled for that rare spice. I loved those rides, they made me appreciate my own luck and happiness, seeing the poverty all around. Because how soon we forget! We grow used to our lives and forget where we've come from. I'd tell myself again and again with a shudder that any one of those barefoot boys squatting on the square could have been me.

Father Ali and Lalla Fatima shared that unassailable tenderness of old couples in the twilight of their lives. They were true partners, joined by an intimacy from which I sometimes felt excluded. One moment he'd be roguishly eyeing up the cook's ample haunches as she stood up from her stool, the next she'd be shivering with horror or laughing out loud and slapping her thighs, at the first story he told. (He had thousands of them, about the ants or bees that crawled into the spout of his teapot, the rats he hunted and where they dug their holes, the snakes—real or make-believe—that he'd behead with one strike of his spade and bury near the well, the canary who'd made friends with the tortoise from the vegetable garden—a whole series of fables that flourished every day in his garden.) The way they carried on left no doubt as to the nature of their relationship, which was more than just the "good friends" they claimed. Catching sight of us through the window, she'd hurry to adjust her headscarf, while Ali made sure to remove his working clothes on the kitchen step. And he'd never come empty-handed; if there were no vegetables to bring from his garden, no fruit or dates, he'd always have a bunch of the mint or absinthe leaves that sprouted all over like weeds.

Father Ali, Lalla Fatima, Sister Odette, and Sister Benedicte had been my real family; I was already missing the School on the Hill.

12

"WHAT'S YOUR LITTLE one called?" asked Kacem Judi.

Nuara looked up and saw that we were all curious to know.

"Sufyan," she murmured.

"That's a pretty name," said the Algerian.

"My sister Tamu chose it."

"I could take him for a while if you like. I'm used to children."

"I'm not tired," Nuara protested.

"Allow me to insist."

She thought for a moment and, deciding it wasn't such a bad idea, stood up and carefully put the baby in Kacem Judi's arms, then went off to stretch her legs. The wind had dropped and the sea seemed less forbidding. The clouds had almost disappeared, revealing the milky halo of the moon where my grandfather's diaphanous face had dissolved. For the first time I felt calm and confident. We bent over to look at the baby, who had woken up. He had beautiful eyes, a turned-up nose, and a full-lipped mouth that smiled at the circle of strange faces. We were suddenly captivated by this wriggling creature who had given us such a fright. Kacem Judi seemed so happy cradling the little mite that when Nuara returned she didn't dare take him again. The trafficker turned his back on us; our interest in the baby seemed to irritate him.

"Eleven months is a long time!" said the Algerian.

Nuara looked at him, intrigued.

"Especially when you're abroad," he went on. "I've known plenty of immigrants who decided overnight they'd never go back home."

"What are you talking about?" Nuara was alarmed.

"He's saying," said Yarcé, "that maybe you're wrong about what happened to your Suleiman."

"How dare you imply such awful things when you don't even know him!"

"Men are all the same," said Kacem Judi tersely.

Nuara shrugged her shoulders.

"I'm not trying to hurt you, my dear, just to open your eyes. I know what it means to lose people you love. It's hard, but you don't die of it."

"You're crazy!"

"Lots of immigrant workers end up—"

"End up what?" she cried out in a strangled voice.

The baby started to cry. She took him back and rocked him in her arms, hugging him tenderly.

"Don't be angry with me," said the Algerian, "but—"

"Leave me alone!"

"Then listen to him," Yarcé insisted. "He's a sensible man, he only wants the best for you."

Nuara bowed her head. Kacem Judi smiled at her.

"Good advice never killed anyone, my dear."

"All I've done for a year now is listen to good advice," said Nuara. "Now it's time to act; I'll worry about the rest later."

"Well said!" exclaimed Pafadnam, who was listening distractedly.

"Your Suleiman might have remarried," said Yarcé. "It wouldn't be the first time, or the last, that something like that happened."

"That's impossible!" declared Nuara.

Kacem Judi patted her hand.

"If he hasn't given any sign of life for a year, anything's possible, my dear."

"Besides," added Yarcé, "he doesn't know he's had a baby."

"Exactly," cried Nuara, in tears. "If he'd been weak enough to take a woman, like you say, he'd give her up the moment he saw his child. If you only knew how much he looks like him!"

"The world's upside down, my dear; over there it's the women who reject the men. If the Frenchwoman found out about you, she'd make him pay!"

"All the same," Yarcé stressed hastily, "it's only guesswork, for what that's worth. We don't wish it on you, we just don't want you getting a nasty shock."

"Whatever happens," murmured Kacem Judi, "you can always count on me. You and the baby."

During her long, painful wait, Nuara had envisaged every possible eventuality, the cruellest obstacles, the blackest misfortunes, and even death. But not once had the existence of a rival entered her mind. How she had cried, imagining her man a down-and-out under a bridge—like the ones he'd described in Paris—after he'd lost his job at the foundry and begun to drink heavily, out of despair; or imprisoned in a dark and freezing cell for a crime he'd been wrongly accused of, or even in a hospital bed, unable to move, after a drunk driver had knocked him down on a pedestrian crossing. She was ready for any disaster, but not for being cheated on with a temptress. Anything but that; no, she'd rather die. Or kill them both, carve them up, tear them to shreds, or sink her teeth into them like she had the dog under the boat. But for now, she knew nothing for sure. The sensible thing was to forget all these stories, concentrate on the imminent crossing and look after little Sufyan. But it was no use, doubts, suspicions, and apprehensions raged on in her tormented heart. France was so far away. She knew the adventure she'd embarked on was full of risks, for her as well as for her baby, but there was no going back. In any case, the European Deportee would surely never give her her money back—money that in truth was only half hers, since it came from the refrigerator that Lalla Maryam had sold to one-eyed Ahmad. Tamu had stolen it one night from her mistress's secret hiding place.

She'd hurried out to join Nuara on the terrace and, flushed with pride at her theft, had proffered the magnificent wad of notes.

"Here, take this, I know you're leaving."

Nuara had almost fallen flat on her back. Nobody knew about her plan to leave. How on earth had the little vixen guessed?

"What are you talking about?"

Tamu smiled her mischievous smile.

"I know everything that goes on in this house."

"She-devil!"

"The four thousand dirhams you've put by won't get you very far."

"So you're going through my things now?"

"You know I can't help myself. The whole house knows. Go on, take the money. Otherwise I'll spend it all on food!"

"Where did it come from?"

"From the sky!"

Nuara frowned.

"It's the fridge money, of course! You think Lalla Maryam would have let one-eyed Ahmad take it away if she'd not been paid down to the last penny?"

"So you stole it?"

"To my knowledge, Uncle Sulei is your husband, at least until we get proof to the contrary, so the fridge belongs to you. Therefore the money from the sale is rightfully yours. And anyway, you'll be far away before anyone realizes it's gone."

Well, it had to be the devil dictating arguments to Tamu, and he too who made them so acceptable to Nuara's ears.

The next day, before dawn, they'd parted at the door of the sleeping household. It was a long and tearful embrace, and, with her hand on her heart, Nuara had promised that sooner or later, come what may, she'd be back to fetch her little sister.

13

A SHOOTING STAR suddenly split the black sky, spreading an enchanted silence through our little group. No need to mention that the wish we all made simultaneously was to suddenly find ourselves on the other side of the sea, over there on the forbidden shore. My eyes met my cousin's.

"I've never believed in messages from the stars," I said, smiling.

"Me neither."

"You're so wrong!" Yarcé exclaimed. "In my country, we ask the sky lots of questions."

"Does it answer?" Reda was amazed.

"Sometimes," Yarcé nodded. "It depends what mood it's in."

"And how do you understand each other?"

"We have people who read the clouds and stars and the wind," Yarcé explained.

"Like the Indians?"

"Yes, like the Indians."

"What do you ask the sky?"

"All kinds of things," said Yarcé. "We turn to it mostly when we're afraid."

"Are you often afraid?"

"More than we like to admit."

Reda thought for a moment.

"What makes you so afraid?"

"Our own demons," Yarcé replied. "Our loneliness."

Reda knew about fear too. Not the rather abstract fear the Malian was talking about, but a very palpable one: the fear of being hit that he'd learned to live with since he was very young. Punishments that end in gangrene and losing both your hands, slaps from bosses in short-lived jobs, kicks from thugs in the street or animals that won't be milked, the sudden swipes of Grandma's stick, the lash of the teacher's whip at the Koranic school, the beatings he took from policemen in the souk; yes, that fear that had pursued him all his young life until, one morning in July, he shipped up at the School on the Hill.

I still remember it perfectly. Father Ali had knocked on my door and announced that, for the first time in three years, I had a visitor other than Mr. Romanchef. "A Bedouin who says he's your cousin," he muttered suspiciously. In one leap I'd jumped off the bed and rushed outside. Besides Grandpa, no one in the village knew my address; all they knew was that I was living in the city somewhere with the nuns. And there's a whole host of nuns in Marrakesh! Yet that had been enough for Reda to track me down. There he was, dressed in a reddish-brown djellaba, his Adidas bag slung across his shoulder, bandy-legged, sheepish, and paling before the spears on the high gate. The moment he saw me he threw himself into my arms. Smiling through his tears he mumbled a few unintelligible words. I was so happy to see him again! His hair was wispy, there was a little fuzz covering his chin and upper lip, and he had a deep voice—more or less: he had really grown up. As I led him to my room, I thought I must have looked like him, the day I arrived. He was a sorry sight, all filthy and ill-looking. Struck dumb by the luxury of my surroundings, he simply patted me several times on the shoulder, then laughed—very loudly. He peered into every nook and cranny, stroked the polished wood of my desk, fingered the mauve velvet of the curtains, opened the wardrobe, whistled, and patted me on the shoulder again.

Before we did anything, I suggested he take a shower, and hurriedly slipped his flea-ridden outfit into a plastic bag. Then I offered him a complete change of clothes: American jeans, a T-shirt, and a pair of espadrilles. As for underpants, I knew he'd find them pointless and uncomfortable so I decided to give them to him later. Reda couldn't get over it: "If I'd known you were this rich, I'd have got away from Grandma years ago!" Standing on a chair so he could see himself from head to toe, he gazed at his reflection in the mirror. Of course, it was all a bit big for him, but he was so overjoyed he flung his arms round me again and hugged me passionately. God how I laughed at the start he gave when he sank onto the bed. He'd come over as dizzy as I had in the old days.

It wasn't till the next day that Reda told me what he'd been through to find me in the three months since he and his twin brother had got to Marrakesh. They had fled the village because as Grandma grew older, she'd become completely unbearable. She fed them less and less, and for no reason would lash out with her stick at whichever of them was within range. Reda worked from dawn to dusk in the fields, while the twin stayed indoors, helping out as far as he could. It was torture. Should he drop a glass or plate, all hell would break loose. The old woman flew into terrible rages, grumbled incessantly, withheld his food, beat him, and swore at him. At any opportunity, she'd shriek that these brats she'd been landed with weren't her son's children at all, that that suicidal bitch had opened her filthy legs for God knows how many dirty bastards, and the fact that she'd been condemned to suffer them day and night was divine punishment. The good Lord, she'd yell, beating her breast, was paying her back for not fighting tooth and nail when she still could to stop that shameful marriage. Her only son, the most respectable man in the village, driven by Satan into the clutches of that slut . . .

Reda had thought of running away more than once, and never dared because of the twin. How could he abandon him in this godforsaken place, prey to that poisonous witch? And taking him away with him was a burden he didn't feel able to bear. When it came, however, the decision to leave had been made one evening, on an impulse. Returning from the fields after an exhausting day's work, Reda had found his brother in tears, sitting on a low wall by the oil press at the entrance to the village. He was so choked with grief he couldn't speak. He was babbling curses against Grandma, swearing by all the prophets he'd never set foot in the house again. Reda consoled him as best he could. Taking him to the shop, he bought him some Henry's biscuits and Coca-Cola. A big bottle all for him. But he had to stop crying. They'd be gone soon anyway, they'd go to El Kelaa, or even Marrakesh. Nowhere could be worse than this hell ruled by that crazy old woman. They'd manage. Aziz was with the nuns; they'd find out where he was hiding and he'd be sure to help, he'd know what it's like getting started. But now they had to go back as quietly as they could, ignore the witch and her abuse, get to their room and go to sleep. The bus fare wasn't a problem, Reda had some savings hidden in a flowerpot on the terrace, enough to live on for a few days while they got set up. And the good Lord would surely take care of the rest.

In Marrakesh, the twin's handicap proved their salvation; having no hands is a precious asset on Djemaa el Fna square. The moment they stepped off the bus a man approached and straight away offered them room and board and what he said was a cushy job. Reda jumped at the chance, he didn't even ask what sort of work the stranger had in mind. We'll see about that tomorrow, he thought. So the deal was struck and the two boys wound up in a house in the middle of the medina, where a dozen or so other boys lived, none of them able-bodied. The full range of human infirmity was gathered in this place. Among the legless cripples and the blind, the boys with harelips or no arms, the twin felt a little as if he'd come home, while Reda for the first time in his life had the delicious feeling of complete superiority over his fellows. Here they learned the kind of work awaiting them: begging on behalf of the man who'd hired them. His name was Sidi Maqdul, or just Sidi. He was a big guy and had a look in his eyes that commanded obedience—fear, really. But as long as Sidi Maqdul didn't suspect anyone of stealing he didn't treat them too badly. He criss-crossed the medina from morning till night; he was everywhere and nowhere, a real ghost who knew exactly what went on within his team. It was impossible to deceive him; those who had dared still bore the marks on their bodies. "Besides," he'd point out, "the more beatings you get, the better it is for business: a black eye, or an eye gouged out, broken arms and legs, my boys, means more money coming in. Just give me the chance to prove it!"

The day after they'd arrived, Sidi Maqdul had begun to teach the two boys the basics of begging. How to bow the head, for example, or coat the voice with tears to excite rich people's pity, how to emphasize a deformity the better to attract attention—all the tricks of the trade that should give a better chance of success. The twin was dressed in rags and let out on the square. As for Reda, he soon learned to limp; he was allowed to keep his grubby djellaba and assigned a busy corner at the entrance to the souk, under a trellis of reeds.

The days passed quickly. The twin was a big hit, bringing in three times as much as his brother, even though Reda dragged his leg as best he could. Sidi Maqdul was the first to admit the disabled boy had the advantage, but he'd still give Reda a slap every evening when they handed over their contributions. At first, the twin had tried to pass his brother part of his takings, but the boss had immediately noticed, and it had earned them both a good thrashing.

Reda submitted to the trials and tribulations of his destiny without complaining, whatever they were. So long as fate didn't settle matters for him, he always took the major decisions of his life on the spur of the moment. And so leaving Sidi Maqdul had been ordained one fine morning when, without rhyme or reason, a tourist had put two hundred dirhams in his bowl. He was an elderly gentleman, dressed all in white and wearing a bizarre-looking pair of sunglasses and a straw hat, beneath which a bald head was just visible. He smiled when he asked Reda what his name might be, and then promised him an equal amount if he'd meet him at his hotel that same evening at exactly eight o'clock. He wanted to take a walk around the ramparts and needed a guide. Smiling from ear to ear, his eyes shining with gratitude, Reda had simply nodded. He'd never seen such a large note close-up: the photo of the king was even more beautiful than the one he saw on posters everywhere, in shops and all along the roads. Clasping it in his hand, he stuffed it deep in his pocket. As soon as the Frenchman had gone, he ran to find his twin in the square and said that they had to run away immediately, go somewhere else, far from Sidi Maqdul, far from him exploiting and beating and terrorizing them, and this whole band of cripples who spent their nights quarrelling and groaning. There wasn't a moment to lose. With the two hundred dirhams they had enough to take the train to Casablanca. That was where the money was. People said the city was so big no one would ever find them there. And anyway, if they were going to beg they might as well beg for themselves. They were trained now: he could go on limping, it was almost second nature and people are so kind to the lame. Between them they could make a fortune. They'd definitely have enough to rent a room somewhere, with a family. But they had to make up their minds right now, Sidi Maqdul might show up any minute.

"Let's go! Get a move on, we're leaving!"

The twin, his head bowed, had let Reda talk without interrupting him once. Then, looking up, he had stared at him long and hard, and at last, in a clear voice, he had pronounced, "I'm staying."

Silence. Reda couldn't believe his ears. His brother suddenly seemed a stranger, no longer the same subdued, shy boy he'd grown up with; three months on the Djemaa el Fna had transformed him. Reda tried helplessly to persuade him, saying that the boss was a crook and a coward who'd drop him at the first sign of trouble, but the twin would have none of it. He said he wasn't up to rushing into another adventure again, he hadn't the strength. He had a roof here, he ate his fill—what more could you ask? Without his hands, he wasn't likely to get very far, and besides, he didn't want to be a burden to anyone anymore. It was time he lived his own life.

His twin had expressed himself so calmly that Reda had no idea how to reply.

"Aziz is with the nuns," he murmured. "I'll find him and we'll come back to get you."

"You can come if you want but I'm not leaving."

"What's got into you?"

The twin smiled and stroked his brother's face with his stump as Reda tried to choke back his tears.

"I'll miss you."

"Me too," said the twin. "Now go, get out of here before it's too late."

Reda had dragged his feet as he walked away. He'd turned round several times, in case his twin had changed his mind. Then he'd come running back and hugged his brother to his chest. He hadn't said a word, for he knew that the least sound would have released the torrent of sobs stuck in his throat. The twin didn't speak either; he too was overcome by sadness but, strangely, he didn't show it.

The sun was beating down on the square as the two boys parted.

14

LITTLE BY LITTLE, Nuara had dozed off. Her head, resting on Kacem Judi's shoulder, had reduced him to a statue. He kept his neck and upper body rigid and didn't budge an inch in case he woke her, but he joined in the conversation by blinking or smiling at the corner of his mouth. Yarcé had started asking each of us what we wanted to do when we got to France. We hesitated at first, but as he started to reveal his own dreams our tongues had begun to loosen.

In his late master's house, Yarcé had got to know a number of wonderful people, mostly artists. The riad was never empty; as soon as one group left, another descended with great fanfare, from England, France, Spain, America, or other countries. Those parties hadn't their equal anywhere in the world: the musicians played their music; the poets recited their quatrains; the comics did their routines; and everyone drank, smoked, danced, and flirted the night away. His late master would dress up as a Moor in a Chinese silk turban, a large embroidered gandoura, and soft leather slippers. Surrounded by a few intimates, he would take his place under the colonnade that looked out on the patio thronged with guests, between two honeysuckle-covered columns where the pasha must have sat in the past. Yarcé would join the rest of the staff on the kitchen steps and discreetly watch the festivities through the thick branches of the orange trees. Nothing escaped him, and he'd make it his duty to keep an eye on the dubious young Moroccans who'd have been picked up furtively on the big boulevards. As soon as one of them went into a bedroom, Yarcé would spring out like a cat in hot pursuit. There wasn't one of those pretty boys who could boast of pinching so much as a trinket. He made their lives so difficult that some of the ones who stayed the night would complain to his master.

All that was so far away now ... But not everything was lost. Yarcé still had an address book filled with prestigious names. Because he used to have a bit of a joke with the people he massaged and indulge most of their whims, many of them had invited him to come and spend the holidays with them. Something which, a few months earlier, had seemed a distant, fanciful dream was now a hair's breadth from coming true. He was determined take his illustrious friends at their word; as soon as he reached Paris he'd get in touch. Maybe one of them would agree to take him on? Or at least recommend him to people they knew? Yarcé was confident: whatever happened, since his hands were his livelihood, he'd never go hungry or cold. There'd always be bodies needing to feel better.

Pafadnam was next to reveal his plans. He was hoping, at the start, to help his cousin sell fake Lacoste polo shirts in the Mantes-la-Jolie markets. It was a lucrative business, the ins and outs of which he'd soon learn. The crocodile badges came from southern Italy, apparently, and the polo shirts from Chinese sweatshops in the thirteenth arrondissement in Paris. The whole lot cost nothing to buy and was sewn together and then sold for a small fortune at markets in the big suburbs. Still, it was quite risky, and he didn't want to spend too long in that business; his cousin had been picked up by the police. He was always let off with a fine, thanks to his valid residence permit, which he owed to the curvaceous white creature he'd had the luck to marry almost the moment he'd arrived in France, and whose photograph, in a short dress with a plunging neckline, had done the rounds of Ségou and the neighboring villages, making all his mates drool with envy. But if he, Pafadnam, were to be caught, he'd be taken straight back to the border—which was why, as soon as he'd made a bit of money, he'd go and find a less exposed, quieter job: nightwatchman in a hotel, for instance, or dog-handler in a parking lot, or nightclub bouncer, or security work in a hypermarket, as his cousin had suggested. Then, as soon as he could, he'd send for his wife and children like he'd promised. Oh, he knew it wouldn't happen overnight, that it would take months, long ones, maybe even years. Never mind, he felt ready for the great adventure. Work didn't frighten him and there were no limits to his patience.

He'd hardly finished dreaming aloud than all eyes were on me. I suggested Yussef tell us his plans. He didn't have any. He said he was ready to stick with any one of us who'd have him, pointing out that he wouldn't be a burden, that bad luck didn't cross over the sea. He was bound to have better luck on the other side. Then he fell silent and looked at the ground.

As a rule, I don't like telling people about my life, for the good and simple reason that there's nothing exciting about it, nothing to interest anyone else. But, caught up in the dynamic of confiding secrets—that mysterious urge that sometimes possesses people who've been thrown together and makes them open their hearts to strangers they'll never see again, the irrepressible need to entrust bits of themselves to unknown ears before turning their backs and going somewhere far away—I began to tell them how the idea of leaving had stolen into my mind, monopolizing all my thoughts as it grew, like a virus that could wipe out all my dreams except one, the dream of departure.

The night before the baccalaureate exam, Sister Benedicte had abruptly breathed her last. No illness, no warning. It was as if the good Lord had decided, on an impulse, to summon her urgently to His side. We'd all woken up one morning, except her. Sister Odette had got worried and at about nine o'clock had decided to knock on her door. No answer. She'd tried again; nothing. Her hammering had echoed down the long corridors and the embroidery room, to the kitchen where Father Ali, Lalla Fatima, and I were drinking our coffee. With dull eyes and a faltering voice, Sister Odette hurried to join us and share her anxieties. Perhaps she'd been taken ill, in which case we'd have to force the door that Sister Benedicte had the bad habit of double-locking.

"At our age," she added, "one should make sure never to lock oneself in anywhere!"

Father Ali rushed to fetch his tools, then we followed Sister Odette to the first-floor rooms. Within minutes, with the dexterity of a professional burglar, the gardener had dismantled both lock and bolt. As she entered the room, Sister Odette said a prayer. She went over to the bed and felt her old companion's pulse. Her hands were trembling, and fear made her carry on praying out loud. As for Lalla Fatima, she'd barely had time to let out a scream before Sister Odette cut her short: "None of that here, please!"

Sister Benedicte was lying under a white sheet, her eyes closed, her face relaxed, noble and at peace. In her hands she held a cross and on her bedside table lay an open Bible.

We were speechless, unable to take in the loss we'd just suffered. No matter what you do, death always catches you unawares. Even when you know it's near, even when you can read it on people's faces and in the way they look at you. We all cried, of course, first on our own and then in each other's arms. Sister Benedicte had died in the middle of the night, as discreetly as she'd lived, without disturbing anyone, in silence.

When I failed the baccalaureate, the death of my second mother obviously had something to do with it. I'm not looking for excuses, I've never tried to dodge the issue to justify my mistakes or inadequacies, but as God is my witness, a layer of crass ignorance settled across my memory after that. I couldn't remember anything anymore, so, utterly disheartened, I had to withdraw from the last exam. On the road back from the Lycée, cars, bikes, people, and animals streamed past me, encircling my sorrow. Isolated, as if an invisible cocoon had cut me off from the rest of the human race, I walked on, helpless, in despair. Father Ali was in the garden, Lalla Fatima in her kitchen. The embroidery room was closed "due to bereavement." Returning to my room like a sleepwalker, I lay face down on my bed and wept like a girl all afternoon. All of a sudden my little world—so peaceful and reassuring—was collapsing, pulling down with it all my hopes and dreams, everything that was good in my life. Just before she'd died, Sister Benedicte had called me into her office to announce that the headmaster of the Victor Hugo Lycée would support my application for a bursary to study in Toulouse. She'd told me how proud of me she was; I'd always lived up to her confidence in me, and she'd do everything in her power to get me a passport. She'd send a letter to her friend the governor. It would all be arranged, as long as I passed the exam, which she didn't doubt for a second I would. Then she'd hugged me tenderly and kissed me as a mother kisses her child.

And now it had all gone up in smoke!

Sister Odette had aged. Her once radiant face, suddenly overcome with weariness, had begun to sag. She hinted at her longing to go home to Alsace, to the convent of her girlhood. She'd be bound to miss the sun, Father Ali and his flowers, Lalla Fatima and all the temptations she put in her way—and me too, of course, the last arrival, who'd occupied such a big place in her and Sister Benedicte's hearts. The girls learning embroidery could take over; the school was running fine, it just needed a little willpower from someone for life to return to normal. The place would be run by Moroccans, of course, but she'd see to it that everything remained as it was. No need to worry about our future.

Sister Odette's reassurances were no use; all three of us knew our wonderful adventure was over. Father Ali wanted to go back to Mgouna, where one of his brothers still lived. The last he'd heard, two years ago now, was that he had some land in the Draa valley where he grew flowers; Father Ali could help him out. There were greenhouse gardening techniques he'd be happy to teach him—he'd learned them himself from Sister Odette, who had lots of books about plants. After her embroidery lessons she'd often come out and sit under a tree with her beautiful flower books, which showed every variety you could imagine. Father Ali would readily trade his wealth of knowledge for a roof over his head and some bread and olives.

He'd asked Lalla Fatima to go with him, if her heart was willing. Between them, they'd be sure to find a little place for themselves in the South he loved so much, and where, in the end, he'd spent so little of his life. People there were simple but close; being so near to the Sahara made them stick together, as if joining forces against the ever-encroaching vastness of the desert. Yes, Lalla Fatima would definitely love it there. Had she heard about the rose festival? Oh, it would make him so happy to show it to her: the streets all strewn with petals, the rose water raining from the roofs and windows, the otherworldly songs, the raucous drum rolls echoing across the mountains, setting the sky and men's hearts aquiver. Then, in late spring, he'd take her to the date festival up in Imilchil. The whole country would be there; men and women came from all over to be married. Perhaps they should as well? Normally, the young suitors didn't know their future wives, but they had the advantage of thirty years; no risk of nasty surprises for them!

Father Ali spoke fervently, his eyes shining and his rough hands flying in all directions. Lalla Fatima lowered her eyes like a young girl standing before her father on her engagement day. Her cheeks were flushed; the fact that her silence lasted so long meant she consented. I don't know why Father Ali insisted on making his tender declaration in front of me—maybe he wouldn't have dared otherwise, or maybe I was the only person close to them both? Turning to me with a fatherly smile lighting up his crumpled, weather-beaten gardener's face, he said in the gentlest of voices that when my conquests and wars and travels were at an end, when the moment came for me to put down my bundle like them, I could always do so in Mgouna. For as long as God allowed, there'd be a home waiting for me there.

It was around that time that Reda turned up at the School on the Hill. All the order, serenity, and sweetness of life were only on the surface by then. Sister Benedicte was dead, Sister Odette about to leave. Father Ali and Lalla Fatima had their bags packed and tied up with string for a long journey. Whereas I was just waiting—for a miracle, I suppose. I was waiting for another Mr. Romanchef to ride up on a white horse with a magic box full of promises. Yes, and I was waiting confidently, however hopeless the situation, because my dreams at least were still alive; untainted by bitterness, they continued to fly up there in the skies of freedom. Arms folded, watching the credulous way my cousin looked at me like the answer to all his prayers, I waited.

And then there was light!

One evening, there was a knock at my door. Reda ran to hide in the bathroom. I opened the door. Sister Odette appeared with her thick glasses and always kindly smile. I had trouble hiding my surprise; she hardly ever came to my room.

"I hope I'm not disturbing you?"

"No, Sister, not at all."

"Can I come in for a minute?"

"Of course," I said, moving aside.

She came in, her eyes taking in the litter of my books and cassettes, my postcard collection. She picked up a few and looked at them closely.

"Italy's such a beautiful country!"

"Do you know Italy, Sister?"

"Only Rome. I went there once to kiss the Sovereign Pontiff's hand. It was unforgettable . . ."

Sister Odette looked dreamy for a moment, then collected herself.

"I've had a letter from the Lycée. The news isn't good."

"I know, Sister."

"The headmaster says there's been a mishap . . ."

I bowed my head.

"Still, in view of your excellent results throughout the year, you're being allowed to repeat the year. You're very lucky! Our dear headmaster seems to think highly of you."

"He's a good man, Sister."

Sister Odette held out a fat envelope with the words *Aziz: Studies* written on it. I recognized the beautiful, round, well-spaced hand of Sister Benedicte.

"This was found in the wardrobe of my late sister, may God rest her soul. I imagine it's money to go toward your education. Here, make good use of it, my boy."

I didn't dare take the sacred, the miraculous envelope that at a glance looked to contain a small fortune, maybe even foreign currency. Sister Odette urged me to accept it and at last I gave in to her delicious insistence. Then she stayed to talk a while about her native Alsace, which she'd left so long ago. She was a little apprehensive about going back to her people, the Lord having called most of her old friends to His side. And she'd developed some very bad habits, too, from this lazy life in the sun, surrounded by flowers and all of our affection.

Sister Odette spoke softly. I was only half listening; my mind was already busy trying to calculate the amount I held in my hand. She'd barely left the room before I settled down on my bed to count my treasure carefully, my Bedouin cousin staring at me in bewilderment. There were twenty-six five-hundred-franc notes. I counted it in my head first. Unable to believe the outcome, I decided to try multiplication. I took a pencil and a bit of paper and repeated the calculation several times, only to find confirmed the superb, the fabulous round figure of thirteen thousand French francs!

Aziz: Studies, the miracle proclaimed. But in this unexpected envelope there was enough to buy the most prestigious diploma with hard cash!

Reda hadn't made a sound. He was looking wonderingly at the booty scattered around me. It was the first time he'd seen such crisp, smooth beautiful banknotes that looked nothing like the faded, crumpled rags of our national currency.

Suddenly he looked up, stared at me, and, in a barely audible voice, said, "What if we left for France?"

15

THE JOB OF go-between was the least exposed part of the trafficking network. Since the three-year stretch he'd done in Fresnes, Momo had refused outright to take the slightest risk. He stuck to touting for would-be immigrants wherever he could, winning their sympathy and confidence and collecting the money for the crossing one week, at the latest, before the off. Anything else, he didn't want to know.

In the month we'd spent in his company in the Café France, a curious relationship had developed between us. Momo was one of those crooks with an unusual gift for friendship, a shark you become attached to even when you know full well he'll end up robbing you blind. In all good faith. What did we care? He described the other world in such detail and so vividly that he made it seem as if it was one of our own memories—from a former life, or a dream. We'd roar with laughter at the scrapes he'd get into and then suffer his setbacks with him, especially the years he'd spent behind bars, which he blamed on that dream, that nightmare, which had haunted his sleep and persecuted him remorselessly, night after night, since his arrival in the promised land. Momo had got himself caught in Paris in the most mundane and stupid of ways. This guy who never let down his guard for a second, even when he was asleep, had been picked up running a silly little errand.

That morning, like every morning at around ten o'clock, Mr. José had sent him out to buy cigarettes from the bar-tabac opposite. Momo used to like this little break from the stench of cod and fried food, from the damp of the back kitchen that seeped into everything. He'd taken off his apron and washed his hands. In the backyard, next to the dumpsters, Joel was vegetating—Joel the permanent fixture, the restaurant's appointed tramp, a mountain of bloated, scarlet flesh stitched into grease-stained rags. One of Momo's jobs, and his alone, was to take the poor devil his daily bread—boss's orders. It was a duty he carried out with good grace, often lingering for a chat with his friend the bum.

In spite of his physical ruin and permanent drunkenness, Joel's mind was all there. He hadn't been born on the street, or grown up there, either; his decline had only come late in his life, just at that age when everything seems settled and people imagine they're safe from fate's dirty tricks. Yes, strange as it might seem, Joel had belonged to the land of the living. Momo found it impossible to picture him as a sales representative for a vacuum-cleaner company, however hard he tried. Yet Joel had had a wife and children, a dog and cat, a car, and even a nice little house in Bourg-la-Reine, bought with a loan—a long, painful loan, extended over twenty years. And then, like a house of cards, it had all collapsed: layoff, divorce, alcohol—well, the usual downward spiral. Shuffling from bridge to bridge, from metro bench to pavement, Joel had finally established his headquarters in the restaurant's back alley. It was a dream home, envied by many of the other tramps, and he held sway there like a great potentate. Momo, his next-door neighbor, so to speak, would declare that no one should really feel sorry for him; at least he could freely walk the streets, settle down anywhere with his liter of wine, watch the clouds and the northern girls go by, and poke fun at all the police in the world. Joel wouldn't reply, or not directly. He'd break into convulsive laughter that usually ended in a phlegmy coughing fit and a thick gob of spit expertly propelled against the dumpster wall. Momo stuck to his analysis. One day, fixing him with misty eyes, Joel began to talk to him in an unusual way, almost fluently, without stumbling over his words.

"The day you reach my level of decay, my friend, you'll find that no one will care where you come from, or where you're going, or whether your papers are in order or not. No, they won't even see you anymore. You'll only exist to the extent that your presence mucks up their tidy, perfect world. You'll be a stain, a blemish they'll sometimes toss coins at to ease their consciences. And you'll drink their money. And ruin yourself further. Because they're only waiting for one thing—for you to die, my friend. For you to clear off the streets, the metro benches, the pavements they hose down at night. And you can be sure that if it weren't for the fear of awaking old demons, they'd happily lock you up in a camp. But don't you worry! Our kind is tenacious. These days, we're multiplying before their very eyes. There's nothing anyone can do, to help us or to stop us!"

Momo left the backyard. As it was a market day, the street was full of people. The fruit and vegetable sellers were vying with each other over the quality and freshness of their wares, the second-hand dealers talking up their cut-rate junk, the flower-sellers vaunting their roses and lilacs. A smell of spring floated in the air. Momo crossed the sun-drenched street and went into the café. Everyone knew him there, from the waiters to the boss, even the toilet attendant in the basement, a woman Momo always gave some change to. He headed for the tobacco counter where Mr. Roger's potbelly splayed before him. Deep in the crime reports of *France-Soir*, Mr. Roger put two packets of Philip Morris Ultra Lights on the counter, as if he'd seen Momo coming through the News In Brief column. He took the money mechanically and handed over the change without looking up from his story for a second. Leaving the café, Momo collided with the bulging chests of two burly men who were blocking his path; he guessed their profession at once.

"Your papers, please," said the policeman with the moustache.

"I haven't got them on me, sir."

Momo's legs were trembling; he tried not to let it show. The café owner emerged from behind his paper and volunteered in a loud voice, "Don't worry about him, my friends, he's no problem. He's the little fuzzhead from Chez Albert."

Feeling supported, Momo added, "Just come with me, gentlemen, over the road, I work in the restaurant there; my residence permit's in my wallet."

The policemen escorted him outside. It was a mistake, leaving his hands free, because they'd barely got out of the door before Momo made a sudden lunge and tore off at top speed in the direction of Odéon. He knocked over a couple of stalls, trampling their stuff underfoot as he forced his way through the crowd, turned into rue Saint-André-des-Arts, ran down it in a flash without looking back, took the first right and dived into a building, gasping for breath and trembling all over. In his thin chest, his heart felt like it was going to explode. The concierge's flowery curtain was drawn, so he rushed up the stairs and on the second floor found himself face to face with an old woman who was coming out of her apartment. She had a basket in her hand, which she instantly dropped. She tried to cry out, but her tongue refused to obey, her mouth gaped in a peculiar way, like a fish out of water. Suddenly she fainted and collapsed on the wooden floor. Momo went over and tried to help her up; she weighed a ton. He lifted her old head, rested it on his knees and started speaking to her awkwardly in Arabic, which didn't help matters. Her breath became shallow and there was a look of unspeakable dread in her watery eyes, while her face, deathly pale despite a thick layer of makeup, mutely appealed for help. Momo patted her cheeks, saw she wasn't reacting; her pupils had disappeared, her eyes flipping back in their sockets as if they were trying to see inside her. He decided to knock at the half-open door. No one answered. Clearly the grandmother lived alone. He was about to ring the neighbor's bell when all at once he heard low, angry voices from the ground floor. Without a moment's thought, he pulled the old woman into her apartment, picked up the empty basket and the handbag, and quietly closed the door. It wasn't long before the steps reached the second-floor landing. The doorbell rang. He felt it bore into his heart. He turned to the grandmother; she wasn't going to cause any problems. Momo took a step, a wrong one, and the floorboard creaked. The bell again, insistent this time. His forehead covered in sweat, he stopped breathing. He heard the door opposite open. A sour little voice explained to the policemen that her neighbor must be out, she usually did her shopping at this time of day, the noise they'd heard would be her blind cat Charlotte, who was always knocking into the walls. The policemen seemed satisfied and hurried on up to the third floor. Still, Momo remained on the alert. He cast his eyes round the dark one-bedroom apartment that stank of cat piss. It must have been centuries since the windows had been opened. Fat cockroaches, not bothered in the slightest by the presence of the feeble cat, crawled across the tiled floor of the kitchen, making a detour round the grandmother. Though blind, Charlotte had found her mistress's face and set about carefully licking off her foundation cream, meowing in a bizarre fashion. Once the makeup was gone, revealing a web of wrinkles that made a nest for the old woman's upturned eyes, Momo said to himself she must be at least a hundred years old. He went over to her and tried to revive her again. He searched for her pulse, pressing her neck the way detectives do in American cop films. Nothing. He thought of listening to her heart, but the old woman's chest was so massive he wondered whether it would muffle her heartbeat. Still, he put his head to the soft breasts; the old lady couldn't really be dead because he felt suffused with a gentle warmth that reminded him of his own mother. He stayed lying in this position for a moment. Charlotte came and huddled up against them and, motionless, all three listened to the commotion of the policemen hurtling down the staircase.

Momo felt so exhausted that he dozed off immediately. His nostrils had become used to the acrid, shut-up smell; his heart had grown calm too. He couldn't have said exactly how long he slept his dreamless sleep. When he awoke, he didn't know where he was or really seem to take in the scale of the disaster he'd become entangled in. The heaviness of sleep still offered a respite that unconsciously he refused to give up. The cat had disappeared. The old woman's skin was cold, like the water snakes of his childhood. An old, very old memory came back to him: he was ten, maybe twelve years old. As often on a Friday, he'd gone with the local boys to spend the day at Oued Tansift, a few kilometers out of Marrakesh. Left to their own devices, this wild gang would tire themselves out swimming in the muddy water from morning to night, running, laughing, squabbling, and splashing each other in the blazing heat. Some of them hunted frogs, some fished for minnows, some charmed the tourists, and followed them into the palm grove for a few dirhams. But what Momo loved was the snakes. It was so easy to catch them in the water! He'd take a whole lot home, hiding them under his shirt, right next to his skin. He did that for years without one ever biting him. Until that particular day, when he'd picked up a dozen or so of all different sizes before he suddenly realized the danger. A terrible fear took hold of him, rooting him to the river bank. He watched his friends running around, not that far away, and their deafening shouts slowly became unbearable. He was terrified that one of them would end up bumping into him and he had a weird foreboding that this would be fatal. Sensing the blood quickening in his veins, the snakes wriggled against his stomach. Holding his breath as best he could, Momo did not move. Carefully unbuttoning his shirt, he sat down on the ground and, his heart pounding wildly, his hair standing on end, he waited for the creatures to go. The minutes seemed never-ending. The last of them slithered into his trousers, brushing against his penis, then slowly inched down his feverish leg toward the damp mud.

Coming round, Momo was horrified to see that the old woman's heavy, creased breasts had fallen out of her undone blouse. He was angry with his absurd erection, stood up, went to the window, and checked that the street was quiet. No sign of a policeman or any suspicious-looking passers-by. A pang of hunger took him to the kitchen, where he ate some bread and cheese. Charlotte came to rub herself against his leg. Her hoarse meowing sounded like an entreaty. He leaned down to stroke her. "We're both alone now," he told her. Then he headed for the door, lit up one of the boss's cigarettes and, without looking back, left the gloomy apartment.

Once outside, he took a deep breath. The sun, showing through a gap in the clouds, gave the winter afternoon a springlike feel. Oddly, Momo's fear had left him. With a light, unconcerned step, he walked on to meet his destiny as if it belonged to someone else.

16

A SUDDEN FLASH of brilliant light, the Spanish trawler's signal came on the stroke of two in the morning. It was like a monstrous bolt of lightning clawing the black night. In any other circumstances we'd have jumped for joy, shouting and hugging and kissing one another. Pafadnam and Yarcé would certainly have danced their funny dance, like they had that evening on the way into the Grand Socco when a troupe of musicians, accompanying a bride's dowry, began hypnotically beating their tambourines. God it was beautiful! On a cart piled high with presents, with oil, sugar, and corn, a dwarf wearing a caftan of gold and silver brocade was prancing about, showing off a glittering set of teeth. Thick circles of kohl outlined his bloodshot eyes, and a mane of henna-red hair hung to his waist. On the same beat, ignoring the laughing onlookers, the two Malians had thrown themselves spontaneously into the crowd. With amazing gusto, they'd executed a furious jig, twisting their bodies every which way in the middle of the circle that formed around them. As the state of trance approached, the musicians had stepped up the tempo, the rattles challenging the tam-tams, their voices joining in a single lament that burst from the depths of their souls. The Malians outshone the dwarf, who let out a continuous ululation; he was delirious, swaying his head, shoulders, and buttocks with demonic agility. Wound round his hips, a bright yellow scarf emphasized the curvy little rump that he wiggled so extravagantly that the cart driver, afraid he might fall, decided to stop, bringing the whole procession to a standstill. Reda and I clapped our hands rapturously, spellbound, thrilled—just like now on the cold sand, as we stared at this light cutting through the darkness.

The trafficker stood lost in thought. Pafadnam and Yarcé seemed to be keeping watch, Kacem Judi was carrying Nuara's baby, she was sitting on a bulging bag, whilst Reda, who was having another fit of the shakes, had grabbed hold of my jacket. I'd be lying if I said I wasn't terrified. My heart was pounding the same as everyone else's, but I didn't show it. I was thinking of my good, gentle mother, Sister Benedicte, up there in heaven busy polishing my dusty, lackluster star. Her presence, which I felt deep inside me, gave me courage. I very nearly started talking to her like in the old days, when just the two of us would meet in her office to talk about literature, history, and religion, when she liked to stroke my hair while I recited a poem by de Musset or Verlaine, our favorite poets. Yes, I'd have liked to show her just once the immense gratitude, the infinite tenderness I felt for her, which I'd never dared even let her glimpse, because for a man from the South, any hint of sentimentality is a shameful thing.

I thought of Sister Odette as well, whom I was bound to see again, Alsace isn't so far from Paris. I'd surprise her one morning by turning up at her convent. I'd bring mimosas, honey cakes, cream horns; she loved cream horns so much! I can't believe the good Lord would be angry with her over such a small weakness. We'd send a postcard to Father Ali and Lalla Fatima. As soon as they found a neighbor to read it to them, they wouldn't be able to believe their ears. I could see big Fatima from here, bringing out the whole village with her whooping, while Father Ali held forth, reeling off a whole string of anecdotes that the postcard, passed round, would revive in his memory. They'd pin it up on the wall and think of us every time their eyes came to rest on it.

Then I thought of my friend Mr. Romanchef and his visits at night to the School on the Hill. He'd bring me books and chocolate and American tobacco and sometimes he'd go over my math homework. After that he'd sit by my side on the bed, take off his glasses, which he chewed at the ends, and in one leap jump on top of me as if to catch me and his conscience unawares, then start trembling as he stroked my penis. It was the kind of thing cats do, which I thought was funny, because I saw it coming a mile off, and because I never resisted. I never, ever refused Mr. Romanchef anything, not just because I owed him my

new life and new world, but also—and above all—because
of his milky, smooth skin, which aroused such desire in
me, his spicy fragrance you never smelled anywhere else,
and his mouth that was like a pitted cherry. Mr. Romanchef
had the marvellous gift of being able to transform me into
a cock, a huge, awesome cock, which contained my whole
being, all my madness, passion, and pride in its hardness.
Responding to a call from deep inside him, I let myself be
swallowed up body and soul by the corridor of scarlet flesh
that offered itself, welcoming and imploring. And I'd lose
myself in it as you lose yourself in a deep, shadowy, thick
forest, seeking secret folds and hidden clearings, tracking
the spark of pleasure in the sin, the glimpse of paradise, a
cry of shrill ecstasy that we both suppressed when, suddenly still, we lay fused together like a creature with two
torsos, breathless and radiant and fulfilled.

Mr. Romanchef always left in a hurry, hardly saying
goodbye, sometimes forgetting his pretty gilt lighter, or his
horn-rimmed glasses, and even one night his wallet, which
he only came back for the week after. I don't know why he
didn't dare meet my eyes after our encounters; mine were
far from passing any judgment on anyone. But that's how it
was. He was troubled by what he saw as a favor he extorted
from me, and which I had no way of refusing him. Which
was wrong, or at least not quite right. He couldn't know
that our intimate games were a thousand times preferable
to the insipid, miserably lonely ones I indulged in every
night to stall my desires or calm my frustrations. How I

missed him when he was away! My thoughts often followed him without his knowing, out there in the back of beyond. I imagined him teaching a classroom of stunned Bedouin boys, and the idea that one day one of them might take him away from me filled me with fear. I knew only too well that Mr. Romanchef would be telling them about dreams that waste away in captivity, dreams that need blue sky and heat, that carry along in their wake the lucky ones who have the patience and the passion to court them.

One day Mr. Romanchef's visits stopped. Neither the sisters nor I heard any news of him. A month later, when I went back to the village, I visited my old school. The hunchbacked caretaker, who with his whole brood took over the French classroom for the summer holidays, told me that my friend the teacher had been transferred to somewhere in the North, near Tetouan perhaps, he wasn't too sure.

So, gradually, all those around me had disappeared, all those I loved and who probably loved me.

And here in turn is my mother's ashen face joining those of my long-lost ghosts, as if I were on my deathbed. The image I have of her is of a pregnant woman sitting at a brazier, stirring a meatless tagine. Smells come back too: ash, spices, alfalfa, animal dung. I was angry with her for putting up with my father's violence, for the beatings she suffered as well as the blows that rained down on us. I was angry with her for bringing me into this world, her world, marked by her ugliness.

I thought of Grandpa. The news of his death had reached me a year after it had happened. Reda had put off

telling me for ages. When I found out, I didn't even feel
sad. And yet we were so close, the two of us. He didn't
like living out in the middle of nowhere either. He was a
city man, used to the noise, the lights, the smoky cafés,
life's hustle and bustle. To me, his death seemed a relief for
him, a deliverance. At last he was free of his old skin all
furrowed with wrinkles, his worn-out senses that didn't
respond much anymore, his tough old heart, his tomblike
shop, the country people that after thirty years of city life
he couldn't understand. Grandpa was the only person in the
village I had something in common with. Sometimes I'd sit
for hours on a sack of corn listening to hair-raising stories
about his illustrious master, the late governor. He'd tell me
all about the palace and its intrigues, describing the scented
avenues, the vast porticoes, the fountains of oriental ala-
baster, the ceilings with mosaic or painted cedar panels, the
slaves, the fairytale parties that drew all the great and the
good. He was so keen for me to stick at my studies, so keen
that I'd be somebody too one day! I'll always remember the
funny sessions we'd have, when he'd test me on history and
geography. We both knew he was completely illiterate, but
that didn't worry him. He'd take my exercise book in his
wizened old hands, sometimes upside down, and ask me to
recite. Then he'd assess me by ear, according to which pas-
sages I mumbled, and reward me—or not—with a packet
of Henry's biscuits and his blessing.

Grandpa's body had been discovered in his shop after it
had begun to decay. The unbearable smell had made the vil-

lagers force the door. Lying on a blanket on the floor, the old man was holding the photo Reda had given me the day he'd arrived at the School on the Hill, which he'd pocketed while everyone else was busy looting the merchandise. In the photo, Grandpa was posing in full doorman's regalia in front of the palace's studded gates. He was so young. So handsome.

As for the rest of my family, what had they done to be so utterly forgotten? But then what could I do? They were buried in my mind like a handicap, sucked down to the depths of my conscience. Besides, I'd always felt that grievous solitude orphans feel, because I'd known from my earliest childhood that although I'd been born in the wrong place at the wrong time, I wasn't doomed to poverty or ignorance. I was a stranger among my kin, a soul forgotten by the heavens, lost in the mud. "Well, things being the way they are, we must make the best of our lot." That's what Sister Benedicte used to say. When I was properly set up in France, I'd send the family some money. I'd like little brother to go to school too. He must be ten now. My sisters would end up marrying Bedouins and making a home somewhere, but I didn't want little brother to become a shepherd.

"Your papers," growled the trafficker.

We looked at each other, nonplussed.

"What papers?" I asked.

"All your papers. Passports, identity cards, birth certificates, address books: any document that could identify you. Got to be as good as naked there, on the other side."

We started going through our pockets and bags, revealing each of our secret hiding places. Pafadnam and Kacem Judi did nothing; they'd burned theirs long ago. Then we followed the trafficker toward the dunes, to the place we'd hidden, when Nuara was fighting the dog. The trafficker dug a hole in the sand and put our papers in it, buried them and planted a stick on top. He'd burn them tomorrow, probably, when he got back, because a fire could have been seen from a long way off if we'd tried lighting one now.

"Welcome to the harragas!" said Kacem Judi.

"What's that mean?" Reda asked me.

"That by burning our identities, we're joining the ranks of the stateless."

"Like Momo," said Reda.

"Steady on!" the Algerian retorted. "'European Deportee' implies you've already crossed the sea, that you've been all snug and happy on the other side. Not everybody's born that lucky. Some harragas never make it. Better just to say it's one small step on the road to happiness."

"Are there a lot of harragas like us?"

"An ants' nest, my boy, a real ants' nest!"

"I haven't seen them."

"All the same, they're everywhere!"

"What do they look like?"

"As ordinary as can be, my child. Having said that, there are two types, passive and active."

"And where do we come into it?"

"We're active, little one, active harragas, because we've

got nothing to lose. But we're not the most dangerous."

"What about the others? Where are they hiding?"

Kacem Judi turned his head and gestured southward.

"It's time," said the trafficker.

His harsh, mournful voice made me shiver. Four of us got into position to lift the boat: Kacem Judi, Pafadnam, Yussef, and me. I noticed for the first time that it was black—weird color for a boat! In his big green oilskin, the trafficker walked in front, toward the sea. It looked as if he were gliding on the sand. Yarcé was right behind him. Reda took Nuara's bag because she was carrying the baby. A thick cloud had suddenly veiled the moon, but there were so many stars that it was still just as light. The waves seemed to grow rougher and higher the closer we got, and the wind off the open sea filled our clothes. Walking ahead of me, Pafadnam seemed even more colossal than before. I don't know why his presence reassured me—he'd even admitted, one evening in the café, that he couldn't swim. No point relying on him then, once we were out at sea, and yet I had a feeling that nothing bad could happen to me next to such a big, strong, handsome man. Because how could God, having made him that way, have the heart to destroy such a beautiful creature?

We threaded our way between the slippery heaps of seaweed the scavengers had left. With our trousers rolled up, we walked barefoot over the icy sand, through the pools left by the tide. The first little foamy waves began to wash in and break around our ankles, submissive and treacherously welcoming. The trafficker gave a signal to put down the boat, which we did, while Nuara, the baby, and Reda had hung back above the tideline. Kacem Judi explained that we had to wait for the right wave: a little more patience, and everything would be fine! He advised us to get rid of our shoes and bags, anything that might weigh us down, because, when the time came, we'd have to push off with all our might and jump into the boat super quick. The timing had to be perfect. One foot wrong and we'd be in the water. Perhaps, if our gracious Savior didn't mind, Nuara and the baby could get in right away? If not, they'd have no chance of keeping up. We turned to the black shadow. Busy studying the currents, he made no objection, so Kacem Judi took the liberty of settling mother and baby in the boat.

I'd have dearly liked Reda to join them, but I didn't dare ask. Eyes staring blankly ahead, my cousin had ignored me when I called him over to us. Had he heard? Was he in any state to hear anything? I couldn't be sure. I decided to go and fetch him, he probably needed reassuring. As I got nearer, I saw he was white as a sheet, although not trembling all over, and he'd started to stink again. I had a sudden urge to scream and shake him awake, see him conquer his cowardliness, flaunt a son of Tassaout's pride, thrust out his puny chest just once in his miserable life, and face up to that Strait that stood between us and our freedom. Instead, I put my arm round his shoulder and led him toward the others. He went along with me, but I felt he was somewhere else. If I'd turned back he would have too; he wasn't in control of himself anymore.

The waves broke against us as we slowly pushed the boat out, anxiously waiting for a gesture or a sign from the trafficker. The baby's yells rang out just as they had at the very beginning of the night. Merging with the slap of the waves and the gusting, shifting wind, there was something ominous about his crying. Nuara struggled to calm him. The water was already up to the knees of some, the waists of others, as we watched for the wave, the splendid, kindly wave that would carry us out to sea in its mighty ebb. While we waited, the currents harried us, testing us, their insistence a clue to what the high seas had in store. Pafadnam was holding the boat steady all by himself, as it pitched in the vicious swell. Kacem Judi gripped Nuara's arm; her groans were getting louder than the baby's now. The trafficker stood in front of us, straightbacked, unperturbed, as his oilskin floated around him, so that he looked as if he were emerging from an enormous water lily. I had the strange feeling that the oilskin was standing up on its own on top of the water, without anybody inside, that it could collapse at any time.

Just when we saw the massive, ideal wave building in the distance, the moon came out again. I swear by all the prophets that my grandfather's panic-stricken face was etched on it with perfect clarity. The trafficker signalled that we should keep close to him to avoid the breaker's full force. Pafadnam, Yarcé, Yussef, and Kacem Judi launched the boat so hard it was as if they were lifting it out of the water. I couldn't help, because Reda wasn't moving. He was rooted to the spot, petrified. I started shouting at him to move, soon it would be too late, but it was no good, he wasn't listening. Then I took the bad, the disastrous decision to go back and fetch him. There was nothing else I could do; leaving him there amounted to letting him die. No, I just couldn't help myself. I'd hardly gone back three yards when the roller caught me, lifting me high in the sky, swept up my cousin and flung us both with unbelievable violence toward the shore—that cursed shore that had been ours from birth, to which we were forever condemned.

Tossed about like straws in a storm, we'd swallowed a lot of water. My head felt all battered and bruised, but I hadn't given up. The boat was not far off, I could still see it dancing on the waves. I could see Nuara in Kacem Judi's arms and Pafadnam and Yarcé manning the oars. The trafficker was perched precariously on the prow, with Yussef at his feet. I could still catch up with them. But first I had to deal with my cousin, that little worm I'd dragged around with me since childhood. I stood up in a rage, ready to hit him, to beat his anemic little face with all the fury that had been building in my fists for years. That was when I found him lying on his back by a rock, unconscious, his mouth filled with sand and his eyes rolled upward. I felt a crazy fear I'd never felt before. I imagined the worst because he was quite capable of doing that to me, here, in the middle of this freezing night. Yes, it would be typical of him to go and let himself die in the most cowardly, squalid way possible, spewed out by the sea like a bit of junk.

I stood there shivering, helpless. I lifted my head and stared at the moon. Of my grandfather's face, all that remained was a blurred impression. I took a deep breath, tried to pull myself together and started with what seemed most urgent, clearing his mouth of sand. I used a shell to help, carefully scraping his tongue and the back of his throat to let air in. Blood trickled down the side of his face. Then I patted his cheeks a few times. Propping his head on my knee, I shook it hard, making sure not to hurt him. There was nothing, no movement, no breath. He was completely lifeless. Rather than give in to the bitter urge I felt to scream and spit at the sea, rather than stand up and run across the sand like a lunatic, I took another deep breath and let my heart speak to *my blood*, since my heart has always managed everything better than me.

"It doesn't matter if we've missed the boat, we can try another time. And another and another if we have to! It's not as if there aren't enough feluccas. We'll ask Momo about it tomorrow. He'll know what to do, he can work miracles; I trust him completely. Course he's a bit of a crook, but he's not that bad. He's only following the laws of business. Any businessman will tell you they can't afford to have feelings. But he's different. He's got a heart, that boy, I could tell from the start.

"Come on, this is no time to give up. I've still got some money stashed in my belt. I'm not stupid, I didn't spend it all. Listen, you've got to wake up, you know, because I'm not going anywhere on my own. I'm a lot less brave than you think. Anyway, you're the one that got me into this mess. France was over, for me, when Sister Benedicte died. Come on, little brother, don't be an idiot. I don't like seeing you lying in the dirt. Every time you fall over, part of me falls with you. And what about your twin? Did you think for a second about your twin before playing this dirty trick on both of us? Even if he says he's set up down there, in that dump, that doesn't mean we should believe him. I bet you he's waiting for us. He's waiting for us to come and get him out of that bastard's clutches. We're not just going to drop him, are we? Family's sacred! We'll go to France, we'll be the kings of Barbès, every night we'll show that Tunisian's princesses the time of their lives. We'll do better than Momo, we won't work for a boss like that, or get picked up like dogs by plainclothes cops. I'll be your eyes and you'll be mine. We'll look after each other, we'll never split up, will we, little brother? But you've got to get up now. Do it for me. For once in your miserable life, do something for me! It's almost dawn. The sun will be rising soon, hope will come back with the light and run in our veins again. We'll walk into town. If you're tired, I'll carry you on my back. I'm still strong. Even this night hasn't beaten me. We'll sing like we used to, when you used to leave your sheep and come to school with me. Remember? You'd spend whole days messing around outside my classroom window. I always knew you were dying to come and sit on one of the benches, but the caretaker wouldn't even let you in after lessons. Well, look, I know what, I'll buy you one, a beautiful bench just for you. Or a proper teacher's desk made of fine wood, like the one in my room at the School on the Hill. Then I'll teach you to read and write. And all those drawings you used to do in the sand with a stick, you'll be able to do them much better on nice paper with ink in all different colors. Then you can give them to anyone you like. We'll have fun, you'll see, like we did hiding in the cornfields, or rolling around in the stream like puppies.

"Come on, just give it a try! It'll be hot tomorrow, we'll go to the Café France, we'll have a smoke, we'll see paradise in Momo's dreams. He's like a brother, you know. He'll help us, I know he will. If you can't stand the flophouse anymore, we'll sleep somewhere else. There's plenty of places. I hate sleeping with animals anyway, the smell of dung reminds me of the village. We can get a hotel room if you like, with hot water and clean sheets, like with the nuns. Come on, little brother, get up, for the love of heaven, get up!"

Then something like a miracle happened again.

Reda suddenly retched, bringing up water and blood and coughing, and his teeth started chattering, and it was like a firework bursting out of the darkness. I looked up at the sky, the moon was still there, but my grandpa was not. He must have gone to tell the good news to Sister Benedicte, who'd be beside herself with worry.

Soaked to the skin, trembling and exhausted, I cradled my cousin in my arms as Nuara did her baby, and I cried silently.

With a threadlike shadow on top, as sharp as a razor, the boat, which was now just a black dot, melted slowly into the darkness.

17

HOW HAD WE managed to wake up so late? Past midday, shame on us! Lying by the low wall of a luxury hotel's private beach, we were practically asking for a caretaker with a big stick to show up. Because we'd slept clasped together to keep warm, he launched into a string of obscene insults, which I didn't even deign to answer.

Reda was there next to me. Alive. That was all that mattered. He looked at me as if it was no big deal, as if the night we'd just survived had been nothing but a series of hallucinations, a dismal tale made up by a cruel griot. He stared at me with twinkling eyes and smiled. His smile was open and tender and, as it lit up my heart, it grew iridescent like a rainbow. It soared into the blue sky, that smile, where our dreams floated freely, and danced like a drunken bird over the sleeping seas, calling out to the intrepid seagulls, to the sea air we both took great gulps of, to this blessed day that promised so much.

We hadn't eaten a thing since the navel oranges the evening before. We were hungry and thirsty. We roused ourselves, left the beach with its few naked tourists basking under brightly colored parasols, and made for the port. Swept up in its swirling, vibrant, unrelenting hubbub, we made our way through the maze of the white city. In the streets and on the pavements, cars, bikes, animals, and idle onlookers all jostled for space. The world went on turning. No one bothered about us, it was as if we didn't exist, as if we'd never been born. So come on, honestly, what did it matter if we were devoured here, or somewhere else, or on the open seas? Near the port, a row of cheap cafés stood wreathed in the smoke of their open grills. Ravenous people came and went, haggling over the best tables, while swarms of beggars and cats preyed on their consciences, trying to keep out of the café-owners' way. We sat down where there was room and ate some grilled sardines sprinkled with lemon juice. Reda was suspicious at first but then he tucked in. They looked fresh. We drank mint tea and smoked a cigarette, then we left the square and walked around aimlessly for hours. Our bags were probably in Spain now, along with my burnous. One of fate's little ironies, but then life is made that way. The good Lord must have had a lot of fun making it up to entertain the host of cherubs crouching at His feet.

As we walked down the main boulevard that was thronged with people as if night was coming on, Reda stopped in front of an electrical shop. I did too. In the vast, brightly lit window there were several TVs, each show-ing a different channel, plus a screen where you could see yourself, which attracted quite a few passers-by. At first I thought it was the football that had caught my cousin's attention, but the most exciting match in the world couldn't have made him stare like that. He'd taken my hand and was squeezing it very hard and starting to tremble. My eyes stopped on the TV showing a Spanish program. Policemen were fishing out bloated bodies. There was a man and child, weirdly tied together with a piece of fabric, two black men, one white man and a woman with her plaits loose. Their faces were hard to make out, but the trafficker's green oil-skin floating in the distance, as well as Pafadnam's size, left no doubt about the victims' identities.

"Perhaps it's not them!" I said.

Reda didn't answer.

"They fish out harragas from the sea every day, you know. No, it's just a coincidence. There's nothing to prove it's them. Let's go!"

Reda followed me, his arms dangling at his sides. He stayed walled up in silence all that day until evening. I didn't feel like talking either. Anyway, what could I have said? We both knew our companions' journey was over. We knew that if the good Lord had spared us their fate, it was because that was His will. Perhaps He'd only postponed it? Perhaps He had a radiant future in store for us? Nuara and her baby were dead. Suleiman probably wasn't waiting for them. Pafadnam must have been bellowing as he went under. And Yarcé, I wouldn't have been surprised if he'd been singing right till the end. Because in Africa, the more you suffer, the better you sing. As for Kacem Judi, he'd be looking into his boy's hazelnut eyes again, and Yussef into his mute brother's, and his mother's, and his sisters', up there in the sky.

We wandered where the streets took us, each wrapped in his own thoughts. We came to a halt near a mosque where a bearded man in a white robe was holding forth to some beardless young men. His voice was warm and kind. I caught a familiar glint in his eyes. He was describing heaven as eloquently as Momo described Paris. He invited us into the circle. We wavered for a moment, but we were so weary we decided to look for somewhere to sleep first. Slowly we walked away from the little group of listeners. I thought about Sister Benedicte and about my grandfather's, where I'd always go for refuge when anyone was giving me a hard time. If my Sister hadn't already been wed to the Lord, I'm sure she'd have married him up there in heaven; the two of them were like a loving shield protecting me.

How did we manage to wash up once again outside the Café France? It was the very last place we wanted to be, and yet we stopped and looked in through the window. The welcoming smells of mint and hashish wafted over to us. Sitting as usual at the back table, Momo was surrounded by a group of people we didn't know. Sometimes he laughed, and his laughter came towards us in waves, sometimes he turned serious, and his gestures acquired a solemnity that his new friends round the table then copied as they hung on his every word.

We stood in silence for a long time, carefully avoiding one another's eyes, gazing at the lights in the smoke-filled room. A languid love song in a woman's despairing voice crackled over the radio. It was beginning to turn cold.

Reda went into the café first.

East Hampton, 1999

LULU NORMAN is a writer, translator, and editor who lives in London. She has translated Albert Cossery, Mahmoud Darwish, Tahar Ben Jelloun, and the songs of Serge Gainsbourg and written for national newspapers, the *London Review of Books*, and other literary journals. Her translation of Mahi Binebine's *Welcome to Paradise* (Granta, 2003) was short-listed for the Independent Foreign Fiction Prize. Her translation of Binebine's *The Stars of Sidi Moumen* will appear in 2013 (Granta, Tin House Books). She also works as assistant editor of *Banipal*, the magazine of modern Arab literature.

ANDERSON TEPPER is a writer and critic living in New York who has written on international authors for a variety of publications, including the *New York Times Book Review*, the *Nation*, *Tin House*, and *Words without Borders*.